"I can't see you again!" Amanda cried

"What?"

"*Please*, Sam, don't ask me to."

Who was it who said desperate times called for desperate measures? Before she could leave, Sam pulled Amanda to him and lowered his head to kiss her. He hoped she wouldn't struggle, break away or slap him silly.

She didn't. She stiffened at first, then melted against him, unleashing emotion so strong he almost shook with it.

Her hands slid up into his hair, his slid more tightly around her waist. And his dog, Hercule, still on his leash, walked around and around them, tangling their legs together.

Good dog, Sam thought as he tasted her lips again. *We both love her and don't want to let her go.*

Suddenly Amanda broke off, disentangling herself from the leash, breathing heavily. He felt his own heart pounding as if he'd just run a four-minute mile in two. She stared up at him, shock written on her face, shock that he guessed came from the way her body had responded to him. And Sam knew that the body—like the heart—didn't lie.

His body, at the moment, was uncomfortably and blatantly telling the truth. And he was positive she'd felt it....

With over a decade's success in contemporary and historical romance fiction, bestselling author **Elda Minger** is known and loved for her emotionally charged and sensuous stories. "Love is the most powerful and healing force on earth," she says. "I consider it both an honor and a privilege to be working in this genre." Recently Elda was nominated for a RITA award by the Romance Writers of America. *Christmas With Eve*, her second Temptation novel, was a finalist for Best Short Contemporary. Look for more award-winning romances from this talented writer in 1998!

Books by Elda Minger

HARLEQUIN TEMPTATION
590—THE LAST SEDUCTION
614—CHRISTMAS WITH EVE
649—NIGHT RHYTHMS

HARLEQUIN AMERICAN ROMANCE
510—WED AGAIN
531—TEDDY BEAR HEIR
584—BABY BY CHANCE

SHE'S THE ONE!
Elda Minger

Harlequin Books

TORONTO • NEW YORK • LONDON
AMSTERDAM • PARIS • SYDNEY • HAMBURG
STOCKHOLM • ATHENS • TOKYO • MILAN
MADRID • WARSAW • BUDAPEST • AUCKLAND

To Cherry Wilkinson (aka Cherry Adair), my dear friend, my writing buddy, my conference roomie (who never sleeps), and the person who can always make me laugh until my stomach hurts, insisting I look at the bright, sunny side of life when things are at their absolute worst. (And does it with such style, like a female Cary Grant.) This romp's for you.

ISBN 0-373-25765-1

SHE'S THE ONE!

Copyright © 1998 by Elda Minger.

All rights reserved. Except for use in any review, the reproduction or utilization of this work in whole or in part in any form by any electronic, mechanical or other means, now known or hereafter invented, including xerography, photocopying and recording, or in any information storage or retrieval system, is forbidden without the written permission of the publisher, Harlequin Enterprises Limited, 225 Duncan Mill Road, Don Mills, Ontario, Canada M3B 3K9.

All characters in this book have no existence outside the imagination of the author and have no relation whatsoever to anyone bearing the same name or names. They are not even distantly inspired by any individual known or unknown to the author, and all incidents are pure invention.

This edition published by arrangement with Harlequin Books S.A.

® and TM are trademarks of the publisher. Trademarks indicated with ® are registered in the United States Patent and Trademark Office, the Canadian Trade Marks Office and in other countries.

Printed in U.S.A.

SAM COOPER FOUND IT extremely hard to be melancholy right before Christmas.

It wasn't as if he didn't have plenty of reasons. What with his ex-partner having embezzled most of his detective agency right out from under him and hightailed it to parts unknown, and with Sam not having two dollars to his name at the moment, things were grim.

But things had been grim before. And he'd just gotten a lead on his ex-partner that put him in the vicinity of Beverly Hills, near the Beverly Wilshire Hotel.

He now found himself swinging the car he was driving around toward the back of that stately hotel, and admiring the fantastic array of twinkling white lights that adorned the building and the large iron gates. Decorated to look like an incredibly fanciful fairyland, it cheered him for a moment. A sea of twinkling lights in wintry, fogbound Los Angeles.

How could life be that bad, after all, if Christmas was merely three weeks away?

And besides, Sam's philosophy of life was that there was always another adventure just around the corner. It was part of what made him—*had* made him, he corrected himself—so phenomenally successful in his work.

Until Evan, his partner. The skunk.

Now as he maneuvered his—or rather, his buddy

Nick's—black Mazda Miata convertible toward the
valet parking lane, he realized that the weeks before
Christmas had to be one of the busiest times for the
grand old hotel. Which meant traffic. Which meant
waiting. There hadn't been a parking space on the
street, or, cheapskate that he was now forced to be, he
would have parked there.

But financial caution was completely overridden by
his intense desire to see Evan again. To confront his
partner and demand an explanation and, more impor-
tantly, his money.

Therefore the traffic, and the delay, was okay. It gave
him a chance to calm down and observe things. To listen to jazz playing softly on the Miata's radio. And to
think about what he was going to say to Evan if he got
the chance to see him.

Right after he planted a fist in his face.

He was distracted from that satisfying thought by the
shrill little beep of his cellular phone. Pulling it out of
the pocket of his black leather jacket, he flipped the
small phone open.

"Cooper here."

The anxious voice on the other end of the line belonged to his only current client, an elderly woman.
Mrs. Boswell had lost her French poodle five days ago.
Though it was a case Sam normally wouldn't have
looked at, at this point in his life he understood the old
saw about beggars not being choosers.

When Evan had skipped town with all of The Blackthorne Agency's funds, it had seriously damaged the
detective agency's credibility. Many potential clients
had shied away. After all, if two men couldn't seem to

agree on how to run their business, how could the one who was left be any good?

People's fears ran even deeper than that. Sam knew he'd been tarred with the same brush as his partner. Nothing scared people as much as the thought that their money might be in dishonest hands.

He couldn't entirely blame these people. It didn't look good, his partner cutting out the way he had. Sam had resigned himself to building the agency back up again, one case at a time. So, even though this particular assignment concerning a missing pet seemed more suited to the fictional Ace Ventura, he'd taken it.

Fifi, the dog in question, was proving to be an elusive subject. At this point, his job was more to comfort Mrs. Boswell than anything else.

Strangely enough, Sam was determined to find the old woman's pet. And he had a sixth sense that he would.

"No, Mrs. Boswell. I'm sorry. No news on Fifi yet."

Mrs. Boswell sounded frightened, yet resigned. And Sam couldn't bear to have the elderly woman hang up the phone in that state of mind.

"I want you to think about Fifi," he said, striving for a comforting tone. "Visualize her. Dogs think in images and energy, and can pick up on what their owners are thinking. And I have a strong suspicion that someone kind has picked her up and is taking care of her for the time being."

"Wouldn't that be wonderful?" Mrs. Boswell sighed, and Sam could picture the plump matron with her thinning white curls, snugly wrapped in her pink quilted robe. Right at this moment she was probably sitting on one of her antique French sofas in her jewel-toned living room, beside a roaring fire. "You are such a darling young man to..."

Her words faded, to be replaced with, "I've been thinking of getting my breasts done—"

"*What?*" Now Sam sat up in his seat, instantly alert. Fifi's disappearance called for action, but surely not something as drastic as a breast augmentation.

A *boob* job? At Mrs. Boswell's age? Couldn't the woman be patient a little bit longer?

"The little thing doesn't know how to fend for herself" faded out, and then he heard a low-pitched, feminine voice declare, "Not in this lifetime!"

Sam held the phone away from his ear, disgusted. No matter what the quality or price of a cellular phone, there were times when one caught interference—or worse, other people's conversations. He wondered who he was unintentionally eavesdropping on.

Then he didn't have to look any further, because he saw the beautiful blonde in the beige Mercedes talking on a cellular phone two cars ahead of his.

Sam simply stared. *What a stunner.*

AMANDA HAILEY WAS depressed. *Major* depressed. So depressed that she'd considered continuing driving all the way to the beach, pulling her beige Mercedes over to the side of the road, getting out and taking another long, thought-provoking walk along the Pacific Ocean. This gloomy, foggy night in the City of Angels matched her mood perfectly.

She had also considered ditching the party she was supposed to be attending at the Beverly Wilshire Hotel tonight. The party she was already late for.

Everyone her mother knew would be here this evening, to help Libby Hailey celebrate the upcoming Christmas Eve wedding of her only daughter. But did it matter that said daughter didn't even know if she wanted to get married?

She knew the answer to that one. *Nope.*

So she'd called her best friend, Cindy. And was trying to articulate her feelings as she waited in the long line of cars for valet parking.

"I don't know," she said finally. She and Cindy had been going over all the reasons for her feeling badly, except the most obvious: even though Cindy was her best friend, Amanda still hadn't been able to confide the fact that, the closer her wedding got, the more depressed she became.

Maybe you don't really want to marry Marvin...

Amanda squelched that notion the moment it surfaced. Guilt, familiar and crushing, threatened to surround her at just the thought of letting her mother down. She owed her parent big time, and not a day went by that she wasn't reminded of how huge that emotional debt was.

"Maybe it's just me," she said. "Maybe I need a change. I've been thinking about making some changes. Marvin's been hinting that I'm a little...lacking up front." She plunged ahead. "I've been thinking of getting my breasts done."

While Cindy remained silent for a moment, Amanda fidgeted in the butter-soft leather seat. Her best friend had a bullshit detector that was beyond compare, so it didn't take long for her to volley back a reply.

"Not in this lifetime! Color your hair with an herbal rinse or even get your navel pierced, but don't start implanting synthetic substances that close to your lymph glands!"

Cindy was a health nut, no doubt about it.

Amanda carefully inched her Mercedes forward, only four cars away from the valet parking. She would be late for tonight's affair. Her mother would not be happy.

"Have you ever considered," Cindy continued, "that the source of all your problems, all this depression, might be your upcoming wedding to Marvin?"

"Oh, Cindy, I don't want to get into this again."

"Well, we're going to, 'cause I'm going to talk to you until I'm blue in the face in order to convince you you're making the biggest mistake of your life. Your mother won't have to live with Marvin Burgess for the rest of her life, but you will. And I don't think you've considered just what it is you're going to be doing to yourself this Christmas Eve."

"Cindy—"

"Don't you think it's a little strange that your mother hasn't invited me to the wedding? I think she's afraid I might just open my big mouth and confront her about what she's doing to you. It has nothing to do with your happiness and everything to do with what kind of show she can put on."

Amanda didn't know what to say. She had a horrible feeling, deep inside her gut, that Cindy might be right. Her mother saw this wedding as the height of her achievement as a "personal lifestyle consultant." But at the same time, Amanda had already determined that she was going to marry Marvin. It was the only way she could see of finally escaping the controlling, manipulative tentacles of her mother, Libby.

Oh, and that little matter of guilt. Her mother was a master at using it. Libby Hailey certainly didn't want Cindy at the wedding, or anyone who might take it into their head to talk Amanda out of walking down that aisle.

"Cindy, knowing my mother, she's probably worried that you're going to try and tell her or one of her friends about the benefits of either garlic or high colonics."

"As if! Getting her colon blown would be the best thing your uptight Mom could do for herself. I just wish she'd stop masterminding your life."

"Marvin is—"

"Old enough to be your father, for one!"

"Well, I guess he is kind of a father figure. But we've talked, and agreed to this arrangement—"

"Oh, *Amanda!* The only *possible* reason you can even be *contemplating* going through with this is because you've never really been in love."

"Cindy, please don't start—"

"I'm going to start, finish, and continue right up until Christmas Eve. I couldn't live with myself if I didn't do *something*—"

"Cindy, you can't possibly still believe in love, like love at first sight. Do you? I mean, that kind of love where you see someone and you just *know*. Do you really believe it even exists?"

"That's your mother talking," Cindy said.

Amanda hesitated. In her heart, she knew her friend was telling her the truth. Cindy rarely did anything else.

"How would I...know?" Amanda asked quietly.

"You would. You just *would*. And you wouldn't be having these doubts. You'd be happy."

"You've been watching too many old movies."

"Maybe. But remember that movie with Steve Mc-Queen and Natalie Wood? *Love With the Proper Stranger*? All I know is that bells aren't going off in your head when you look at Marvin. And nothing much at all is going on in your heart."

The conversation was hitting a little too close to some truths Amanda instinctively knew she wanted to ignore. She would never be able to get through this evening if she gave in to her feelings.

"Gotta go, I've reached the valet parking. I'll call you tonight. Afterward." And with that, Amanda turned off her cellular phone and focused her attention on the evening ahead.

AMAZING, THOUGHT SAM, *how much information the world of modern technology can put at your fingertips.*

Her name was Amanda. Amanda the goddess. She had a best friend; a good, *loyal* friend named Cindy. Amanda also had a mother named Libby, who wanted her to marry a jerk—a jerk old enough to be her father!—named Marvin. And Marvin wanted a little more up front. But Cindy didn't want Amanda to compromise her lymph glands—

Stop. It's beginning to sound a little too much like One Life to Live.

Back to the facts. The wedding was set for Christmas Eve, less than a month away. And Amanda was having serious doubts about this marriage, because she was depressed enough to consider mutilating her body for this Marvin.

And, best of all, according to her friend she'd never been in love, so she didn't know what she was missing.

Well.

Not only had she never been in love, she didn't even seem to believe in it. Love at first sight. *Coup de foudre,* as the French called it. That lightning bolt. That message to the brain that told you that you were in the presence of a person who could make you very, very happy.

And if she didn't have a whole lot of faith in love at first sight, he would bet what was left of the agency that she'd never even entertained the possibility of lust at first sight. But after all, love had to begin somewhere, and lust was as good a place to start as any.

This woman, this Amanda, inflamed his curiosity in a way no other woman ever had. He wanted to find out more about her, who this Marvin was, what was going on.

Sam believed in love. Growing up around his mother and father, he couldn't have believed otherwise. Theirs had been a love match. Six children later, his father had still brought home roses, taken his mother dancing and been her absolute rock. He still adored her, cherished her and tried, in any way he could, to make her life easier. And a whole lot of fun. Sam couldn't remember a time when he'd been growing up that his entire family hadn't shared a lot of laughter.

And that was what he wanted for himself. The whole enchilada. His mother and father, and their extraordinary relationship, had made an incredible impression on him. And he was waiting for that moment. That woman.

Unlike Amanda, he would *know.*

He wanted it all.

When he gave the matter any serious thought, Sam knew that was why he'd reached his mid-thirties and wasn't married. He'd been waiting for that lightning bolt. He'd dated a lot of women, even considered marrying one or two. But none had affected him in that overwhelming way, caused that pure jolt of emotion he wanted to feel.

Unlike this Amanda, he wanted to be sure.

Now, having seen this woman, this total stranger, he felt something he'd never felt before. And he wanted to see more of her, find out more. If he saw her again, and that same peculiar feeling raced through him—

Lust or love, Sam knew he had to check this out.

He'd turned off his cell phone at the exact moment Amanda had, deciding to call Mrs. Boswell back that evening. The woman was up all night anyway, a total insomniac even before her beloved Fifi had dug another hole under the ornate wrought-iron fence and hit the road. He knew Mrs. Boswell made a habit of sitting in front of her fireplace with a glass of good Bordeaux, devouring the mysteries she bought by the bagful at her local Barnes and Noble bookstore.

But for now, Amanda had his attention.

When she gracefully got out of her Mercedes, she *really* got his attention.

Legs that didn't quit. A shining fall of long, silvery-blond hair. Curves in all the right places. What was this Marvin, a total idiot?

Sam felt himself become light-headed as she brushed a strand of that silvery hair out of that face, took the ticket the parking attendant gave her, then walked into the five-star hotel, all slim-hipped elegance and grace.

She was a dame, all right, in the best sense of the word. Sam loved old movies, and this woman was a cross between a young Lauren Bacall and Audrey Hepburn in her youthful prime. Long, long, coltish legs. Shimmering blond hair. And the sweetest little face, with just a hint of mischief. He suspected she kept that part of her personality tightly repressed, and he found himself wondering if he could coax her to bring it out and play.

Keeping an eye on the large, double doors Amanda the goddess had just walked through, Sam had to smile.

AMANDA ENTERED THE elegant ballroom after checking her faux fur coat. Though her mother would have preferred her to wear the real thing, that was one area where Amanda refused to compromise.

The off-white, sparkling beaded sheath clung to her figure. Remembering her mother's admonition concerning the extremely good posture a woman needed to pull off an outfit such as this one, she hurriedly straightened her shoulders and glanced around the ballroom, searching for a familiar face.

All of her mother's dearest friends, all upstanding citizens of Beverly Hills, stared back, observing her.

Then her mother, fluttering and nervous as usual, always supremely conscious of what other people thought, came gliding across the gleaming floor, a tense expression in her hazel eyes.

The one word Amanda would have used to describe her mother was *polished*. From the top of her perfectly cut blond hair to her expensively shod feet, Libby Hailey looked exquisitely put together. Her blindingly expensive but understated Armani gown practically screamed good taste and restraint.

"We were worried, Amanda. You were running late."

"Traffic." That one word, in Los Angeles, could be used to cover up a multitude of sins, including the fact that she'd dawdled so long in front of her walk-in closet that she'd barely had a minute to spare once she'd hit the road. She'd also been so nervous, she'd skipped dinner.

"You look beautiful, darling, though I do wish you'd chosen to wear your hair up. Marvin's over there, by the bar. Why don't we see if the photographer can get a few pictures of the two of you dancing?"

That meant, *I want a picture of you and Marvin to grace the social pages of the local paper as soon as possible. I love the attention. I love the adulation. I love being important.*

Sometimes Amanda wondered how her mother had ever given birth to a daughter as different from her as she was. The two of them had been like chalk and cheese since the first few days of her life. It had never been easy between them.

As time passed, things had gotten emotionally worse. Libby, a master at instilling guilt, had never let Amanda forget just how much she'd given up as a single mother. Such a sacrifice. Now Amanda felt that soul-destroying little niggle of guilt every time she thought of backing out of this wedding her mother had arranged.

An arranged marriage. In this day and age, it seemed such an anachronism. But, as her mother was ever so fond of pointing out, "Darling, the rules are *different* for the rich." Libby Hailey would have suffered a heart attack if Amanda had fallen in love with a pizza delivery boy or one of the struggling musicians or actors so prevalent in Los Angeles.

As she'd reminded Amanda over and over, Marvin was "an excellent match. *One of us.*"

And after all, Amanda knew both she and Marvin had agreed it wouldn't be a marriage in the real sense of the word. It was a marriage of convenience, a convenient little arrangement. A manner of living so Marvin could have a trophy wife and she could get out from under her mother's controlling influence.

Yet, if all this were true, why did she feel so ambivalent?

AFTER CHANGING INTO THE suit he kept in the trunk of his car—along with several other changes of clothing—Sam found it incredibly easy to bribe his way into the engagement party. After sizing up the large crowd, accepting a flute of very good champagne and eating a few amazingly tasty appetizers, he zeroed in on Amanda.

The woman standing next to her, a shorter replica of Amanda with the same silvery-blond hair, had to be Libby, her mother. Only her hair was cut in a shorter style. Even in heels, her daughter towered over her. Sam estimated Amanda to be about five-ten in her stocking feet.

Fine with him—he topped six feet. Not the most inconspicuous height for a detective, but he'd made it work for him.

But hair color and basic build was where all resemblance stopped. Sam had had a lot of practice sizing people up, and he would have pegged Libby even without the charming description available courtesy of his car phone.

Libby looked like exactly what she was. A master manipulator. A *scared* master manipulator. Sam would have guessed this was not a woman to the manner born,

but a woman desperately trying to find a way to get inside that particular gilded cage—and stay there.

She'd obviously found her ticket in her daughter, because Amanda was stunning. Really something. Sam
could understand how even a moron like Marvin could
want her in his life. She wouldn't be a strain on the eyes,
and he had a feeling that, if she opened up a little and
stopped the scared-princess approach to life, she could
be a lot of fun.

He accepted another flute of champagne, setting
down the empty one on a tray, selected another incredibly delicious leaf of Belgian endive piled with dilled
baby shrimp, then proceeded casually over to where
Amanda and her mother were standing.

And Marvin. The older man with his arm draped
possessively around Amanda's waist had to be Marvin.
And he also looked exactly like what he was. A man so
born to the manner he'd probably never ventured very
far away from his estate—unless he went first-class all
the way.

Sam had him sized up in a heartbeat. He'd worked
for men like Marvin. Typically they wanted a job done
with as little fuss as possible, not wanting to see the
darker, more sordid side of life. Their money bought
them a comfortable lifestyle, one that didn't involve
ever having to slum for a living. Or understand what it
meant to live dollar to dollar.

He'd almost reached the happy group when his instincts told him this was not the time. Veering to the
right, he joined a cluster of society matrons and their
discussion concerning which type of fertilizer was the
best for their prize-winning rosebushes. And of course,
how awful the hired help was these days.

As his mother was a voracious gardener, and he and his five siblings had all been "the hired help," Sam knew his stuff.

Within the hour, two of the musicians finished their soft, cultured violin-and-harp music, and the others joined in. They began to play music that was obviously supposed to get the guests dancing. Sam watched from the sidelines as Marvin led Amanda out onto the dance floor amid a smattering of applause, and didn't like the feeling that started to build in his gut.

But what could he, Sam, offer her, anyway? *Hey, Amanda! Dump this guy Marvin! What can he do for you? Now me, I've got a bankrupt detective agency, and I sleep on a black leather sofa in a single room above a glorified saloon! Hot stuff!*

Sam narrowed his eyes as he watched the couple dance. Another portly man, a real fat cat, cut in, and Marvin smiled indulgently as he handed over his bride-to-be. Sam watched Amanda and this second man continue their dance as he downed the last of his champagne.

Okay. The pursuit begins.

And what a challenge this promised to be.

AMANDA FROWNED, concerned. Archibald Craine, her dance partner, was starting to sweat. Tiny droplets stood out on his flushed and balding head. She wanted to encourage him to slow down, but knew from long experience with Marvin's friends that Archie would take this as an affront to his manhood.

Or what was left of it, at sixty-eight.

She was saved from making a decision by the man who cut in on them. Tall and dark, he seemingly glided up out of nowhere, tapped Archie on one shoulder, then smiled.

"May I?"

Archie goggled, but before he could reply, Amanda felt herself being swept into younger and much stronger arms. Suddenly she was dancing with a stranger.

A very self-assured stranger. Handsome and muscular, though not in a bodybuilder way. She sensed an incredible intelligence radiating from those cool eyes— very cute-guy eyes that were studying her in an intent manner she could feel all the way down to her toes.

Though he'd only touched her lightly when he'd taken her into his arms, there was an intensity behind the gesture that made it impossible for her to take her eyes off him. Feminine instinct kicked in and told her she was in trouble. Big trouble.

He was looking at her in such an intent way. Studying her as if he were searching for something. For a moment, she thought she glimpsed an aching vulnerability, a *yearning* so strong she caught her breath and involuntarily stepped back, away, breaking contact on the dance floor for just an instant.

He eased her back into his arms as if she belonged there, and that peculiarly intent expression on his strikingly masculine face returned. Her heart kicked into overdrive.

"I don't remember seeing you before," she said, trying to keep her tone cool and somewhat remote even though her heart had started to race. This man felt threatening, though she knew he would never physically hurt her. "I'm sorry, have we met?"

"Not till now, Amanda," he said. "I'm Sam Cooper."

"How do you know my mother? Are you a friend of hers?"

The way he was looking down at her literally stole her breath away. She'd never understood that phrase until just this moment.

This man had no place in her perfectly orchestrated little world. And she hadn't a clue what to do.

SAM WAS A MASTER of the outrageous fib in his line of work, but he found he couldn't lie to this woman.

"How do I know your mother? I've seen her television show." And Sam blessed *his* mother for passing on a terrific photographic memory. He could remember anything, and while watching both mother and daughter earlier, he'd suddenly figured out where he'd seen Libby Hailey before.

Libby's World was a syndicated television show in which Libby, the lady of the manor, showed women how to fill their time with...diversions. Drying their own flowers for lovely springtime wreaths. Shearing their own sheep, washing, carding and spinning the wool, and knitting lovely, one-of-a-kind sweaters for their glorious brood of children. Growing their own pumpkins so the kids could experience the wonder of creating their own jack-o'-lanterns.

Libby had become the archetypal goddess of hearth and home. Women across America literally worshiped her and what she represented, behaving like rock groupies at the various events Libby staged at upscale department stores.

And the food! Stews and soups, cookies and brownies, flans and paellas. The freshest ingredients, everything from scratch, complete with gathering your own herbs from the kitchen garden you just happened to plant in your spare time—after you sand-cast the sculpture for the center of it.

Libby Hailey made Martha Stewart look like a dilettante.

And unfortunately, Libby's specialty was weddings.

This, thought Sam, *is going to be a little harder than I thought.*

How did he know all this? His sisters had caught a few of Libby's shows while he'd been back East recently, visiting his large, boisterous family for Thanksgiving. None of them would have had the time to do any of her crafts or recipes. But as his oldest sibling, Thea, had pointed out, "It sure beats watching all that depressing violence on the evening news."

And if Libby was obsessed with growing the perfect jumbo gourd or seasoning a stew just so, then Amanda herself was the ultimate pièce de résistance for a wedding to end all weddings. Sam could see that Libby Hailey thought of her daughter as her own personal Galatea.

But that was neither here nor there. He finally had Amanda in his arms and, he sensed, not for long. She felt and smelled sensational—the chemistry was right—and he had to work fast.

That lightning bolt had struck but good. He'd only needed to get closer, to touch her, to take her into his arms. See her up close, smell her delicate perfume, and that scent that was hers alone.

Something was happening between them, something wonderful. He knew she wouldn't admit it; it would probably frighten her. After all, this was a woman who didn't believe in love.

Then why was she looking up at him like that? Why did she practically tremble in his arms? And why did he *know*, now that he'd managed to get close to her, that she was the woman he'd been waiting for all his life?

Where the hell did that thought come from?

But it was true. The more die-hard the bachelor, the harder he fell. And Sam had waited for, and wanted, this long, delicious fall ever since he'd first figured out the difference between the sexes. Hell, if he had to fall, he wanted to fall hard. Wanted it to be worth it.

This woman in his arms, even with all the difficulties attached to his pursuit of her, was worth it. Instinct told him this, while reason told him that to court her was impossible. As a detective, Sam always went with his instincts. They'd never failed him.

What now?

The first thought that flashed into his mind was, *Never underestimate the value of shock appeal.* It had certainly worked for Howard Stern.

"First of all," he whispered into her elegant little ear as they danced, "you only need one big change in your life. Dump this guy, Marvin."

"What?"

Now he had her complete attention. He smiled down at her startled expression. Even surprised, she had the most beautiful blue eyes he'd ever seen. Eyes he could look at for the rest of his life. Eyes he wanted to make dance with laughter, close with intense passion.

"Second," he said, "forget the boob job. Your friend Cindy's right—and I think you're perfect the way you are."

"Who *are* you?"

Tightening his hold on her so she couldn't run away,

he whispered, his answer a hairbreadth away from her ear. The words that came out of his mouth, impulsive and heartfelt, surprised even him.

"I'm the man you're going to marry."

2

SHE COULDN'T BELIEVE what she was hearing.

He couldn't possibly be serious.

No man asked a woman to marry him out on the dance floor during her engagement party. Well, no one except this Sam Cooper.

He'd effectively rendered her speechless, so she simply stared up at him as they twirled about the dance floor. And insane or not, she had to admit he was a fabulous dancer.

"Amanda, I think you should marry me. I'd get down on my knees, but this dance floor's a little crowded."

"You're crazy," she whispered, looking up at him. Here he was, that mythical tall, dark stranger who had mysteriously materialized out of nowhere. And, like her mother, had decided he had the right to take over her entire life. Well, that just wasn't going to happen.

She had her priorities clear. Nervous or not—and her mother had assured her that all brides were nervous—one thing Amanda was sure of was that Marvin had a busy life already mapped out. Other than showing up on his arm once in a while as the quintessential trophy wife, she had no other duties. Not even sexual ones.

And she would finally have her freedom.

"Crazy in love, that I'll admit," Sam said.

"How did you know about...about..."

"The boob job? Just call me psychic. And from what I

see in your future if you marry this Marvin guy, it isn't going to be a happy one."

"You're sure about that?"

"Absolutely and positively."

He was bringing up emotions she had no control over. Fear. Desire. Curiosity. And that yearning to be free, to fly, to follow her heart, no matter where it led—

She couldn't.

"This dance is over." And with that, she gently disengaged herself from his arms and walked off the dance floor.

HE'D HAD TOUGHER, MORE difficult challenges in his lifetime, Sam supposed as he watched Amanda make her graceful exit. But none as beautiful.

Now with something this crucial at stake, he had to keep a cool head.

Engaged isn't married.

The wedding takes place on Christmas Eve. Three weeks from tonight. He'd learned that from one of the society matrons he'd chatted up, discussing roses and manure.

And her mother is going to be one formidable opponent.

Well, there was only one thing to do. As in any tough case, Sam knew when to cut and run. To gather and evaluate his resources and come back another day. Right at this point, he needed a little more information.

THE DRIVE BACK TOWARD Pacific Coast Highway on the Santa Monica Freeway wasn't pleasant. Angelenos, used to sunny, smoggy weather, hadn't a clue how to deal with, or drive in, thick fog. Sam drove along the freeway cautiously, not even answering his cell phone when it beeped.

He needed his wits about him.

And his thoughts were filled with Amanda. He wondered what she would look like if she really let go and laughed. How her life might have been different if her mother hadn't so clearly wanted to run every detail of it. And how he was going to convince her not to marry Marvin.

Sam had been something of a tomcat during the years his family had jokingly referred to as his "wild youth." His mother had despaired of his ever settling down and giving her any grandchildren. So much so that, last Thanksgiving at his family's home in Baltimore, in the kitchen while he'd been helping his mother clean up, she'd told him, "When you finally find the right one, you're going to fall like a ton of bricks. And the sooner, the better."

Ah, you were right, Mom. As usual. Ton of bricks? More like several million tons of cement.

His thoughts strayed back to Amanda.

She's the one.

He headed on to Pacific Coast Highway with just as much caution, as the fog was always thicker nearer the ocean. Now, squinting against the misty gray swirls and glowing pairs of headlights that seemed to come out of nowhere, Sam headed north up the coast, the ocean a dark presence on his left.

Within half an hour of extremely cautious driving, he was turning left across the oncoming lanes of traffic as he eased the black Miata into the large parking lot of Nick's at Night. The electric-blue neon sign, with the club name swirled around a martini glass that continually tipped over and righted itself, winked on and off against the fog, tinting the gray mist a bright blue.

The jazz club had been around forever, was practically a Los Angeles institution. Nick Mangione, one of his best friends, had inherited the club from his famous father, a jazz musician who had started it. The combination of excellent Italian food, hot music and an incredible oceanfront location had ensured that the club had become a success. Though situated in Malibu, it attracted music lovers from all over Los Angeles for a relaxing evening by the Pacific.

Sam parked the small sports car but didn't go inside the club. He had no doubt that Nick would be there, presiding over the bar, running things with the utmost precision, seeing to every need of every guest. But Sam found he wasn't in the mood for the comfort of a crowd.

He didn't want to blend in and disappear. He didn't want to try and distract himself from his thoughts. He wanted to go up to his room and sit quietly. And try to figure out how he was going to deal with Amanda.

Until this evening, his only goal in life had been to find his partner, Evan, and get back at him. Get back the agency's money. Now he had a different agenda, because that lightning bolt had hit, but good.

Fog curled around him as he stepped out of the car. The booming of the waves and the strong smell of the sea reassured Sam as he locked the car and headed toward the wooden stairs at one end of the club. The wood had been bleached by sea and sun to a pale, silvery color. Now Sam mounted the steps, taking them two at a time in his haste to get to the third floor and inside. Though he loved the ocean and all its changing moods, tonight felt chilly.

He walked along the generous balcony, then unlocked the door and stepped inside, welcoming the warmth as he turned on the light. Soft illumination revealed the one large room he now called home.

About twelve by twenty feet, it housed all he owned in the world. Several bookshelves crammed with books and videos. Two large file cabinets filled with files. A large-screen TV, a stereo system, a scarred desk that held a formidable computer system, and, of course, the long black leather couch he now used as a bed.

The view depressed him. What could he possibly offer Amanda? She probably lived in a mansion in Beverly Hills, while he was reduced to one room.

Why had he fallen for his complete opposite? What could he, at one of the lowest points in his financial life, offer a woman like her?

Then he thought of his mother again, always up to her elbows in either garden topsoil or bread dough. She'd been the consummate homemaker, and had only wanted to create a home that ensured her husband and six children were happy. Sam knew exactly what his mother, the ultimate romantic, would tell him.

You can give her love, Sam. Lots of it. You can love her better than anyone else on the planet.

This was true.

The down sleeping bag on the couch wiggled, and a tiny little canine face, all wrinkled and pushed in, wormed its way out from beneath the bag's folds.

"Hello, boy," Sam said softly. Poor Hercule, his French bulldog, hadn't taken their move well. The puzzled, sad expression in his bright little eyes told Sam he still didn't quite understand what was going on.

Sam had found Hercule while working on a case about two years ago. The little dog had been sitting on the side of the road, an attitude of defeat in the way he'd been slumped against a cinder-block building. Some children had been pelting him with stones as Sam had exited the apartment complex across the street.

He'd wrapped the little bulldog in his coat and taken him straight to the vet, then paid a large bill he could hardly afford. But something about the animal, and how he had been resigned to his fate, had touched Sam deeply. So much so that his original plan—to find the dog a good home—had metamorphosed into Hercule moving in with him.

He was good company. Unlike most bulldogs, he rarely snored, and he liked a lot of the same things Sam did. Good food, old movies and the occasional walk along the beach.

"Well, it's cold outside, buddy, but we've got to empty you out."

Hercule gave Sam an injured look, then hopped off the couch and walked over to the door. Sam snapped on his leash and took his dog outside.

Within twenty minutes, with Hercule snugly situated in the one large easy chair in front of the television and a video of *Casablanca* beginning to play, Sam sat down at his desk and turned on his computer.

The first thing he always did on a case was gather as much information as possible. And though Amanda Hailey wasn't technically a case, he had a feeling he needed to know a lot more about this mysterious woman before he took action. So he had to create a file on her.

As a private investigator who was totally at ease with both computers and the Internet, Sam knew how to build a complete and thorough dossier on anyone on the planet. Though his customers had abandoned what they'd perceived to be a sinking ship, he still had his loyal sources and contacts.

Between the data he could bring up on the computer and what several carefully placed phone calls to people who were experts at digging out information could produce, Sam knew he wouldn't have much trouble. For this particular case, he would call a few of his contacts in Beverly Hills and Bel Air. Maybe Pacific Palisades. Oh, and anyone who'd worked at the studios on *Libby's World*.

Investigating Amanda Hailey's life up until now wouldn't be that hard. Neither would that of her mother, Libby. Especially Libby. Sam had a feeling that the woman loved her brush with fame. There would be articles about her and her show. People she'd worked with. It wouldn't be that hard.

And the best friend. Cindy. It wouldn't hurt to know something about her. The woman's last name would probably come up somewhere in Amanda's life.

Scooting his office chair along the floor until he reached the refrigerator, Sam pulled out a bottle of beer. Opening it, he wheeled himself back to his desk and set to work. It was going to be a long night, but he had a feeling it would be time spent that would yield results.

"YOU SEEM VERY QUIET tonight, darling. Is everything all right?"

Amanda knew better than to answer her mother. She simply concentrated on driving along the tree-lined streets of Beverly Hills. What Libby really meant was, *Is everything still proceeding according to plan? And it had better be.* She could feel the beginnings of a tension headache forming. All she really wanted to do was run up to her room, take a few aspirin and go to bed.

Anything to wipe out the image of Sam Cooper. Somehow, no matter how he had irritated her, she couldn't seem to get him out of her mind.

"Who was that man you danced with tonight?"

Her mother was sharp; Amanda had to grant her that. She didn't miss a thing.

"I thought he was a friend of yours." The best defense was always a good offense. She shot the ball right back into her mother's court.

"I've never seen him before in my life." Libby paused, playing with the opulent ruby-and-diamond cocktail ring on her finger. Amanda knew the next comment she made would probably be upsetting. Or invasive.

She wasn't disappointed.

"He seemed to irritate you. You appeared upset when you walked off the dance floor."

"Not at all. I just needed some air. It was rather close among all those people."

"I see."

Those two words told Amanda her mother still hadn't let go. Amanda rather enjoyed the fact that Sam Cooper had irritated her mother. It was something she herself had never quite found the courage to do.

Oddly enough, that was the one thing that made her like the man.

"Marvin was in a good mood tonight," her mother remarked.

Oh, yes. Marvin. Amanda knew that one of her main jobs, if not the main one, was to keep Marvin Burgess happy as a clam until she walked down the aisle and became his bride. This irritated her, because she knew he rarely thought of her. Marvin's life was Marvin's first priority. As long as she didn't cause any trouble and showed up on his arm, letting everyone know he still had what a young woman wanted, he would be content.

Her mother was making this more trouble than it was.

"Yes, he was in a good mood," Amanda said quietly.

"Things are going well for him?"

She hadn't a clue, but wouldn't let Libby know. "Yes."

"Darling, you looked so lovely in that dress tonight."

"Thank you." For one moment, Amanda desperately wished she could take her mother's compliment at face value. How wonderful it would be to have a mother who truly thought she was beautiful. Special. But she knew Libby was merely concerned about how she appeared to others. To Marvin. And how that reflected on her.

Amanda knew her mother was self-centered. Libby Hailey had never possessed even a speck of the compassion and self-sacrifice many mothers came to instinctively. For years, Amanda had fought against this truth, until one day she had merely given up. Two days later, her mother had introduced her to Marvin. Within six weeks, Marvin had proposed. Amanda had accepted, her only goal to leave her mother's house and finally start an independent life of her own.

To most people, this marriage of convenience would have appeared ludicrous. Here she was, a young woman of twenty-four, almost twenty-five. Perfectly healthy, with her whole life in front of her.

And perfectly incompetent.

For Libby had sheltered her to an extreme degree. Amanda had never had to make even the most elementary of decisions. For years, she'd gone to her mother's stylist on Rodeo Drive, and had her hair cut in a style that pleased Libby. Her mother had picked out her clothes, her friends, even her classes.

She'd had what others would have considered a privileged childhood. Private schools, trips to Europe. Carefully planned parties where only the "right" people were invited. Plenty of money at her disposal, though Libby had always carefully held the purse strings—and the whip hand.

Amanda didn't consider herself a stupid woman. Far from it. She'd taken several psych classes in school, and realized she'd barely scratched the surface of life. She really hadn't a clue about what lay beyond the high gates of her mother's estate. There was a whole wide world out there, and she hadn't seen a bit of it. Just the carefully controlled parts her mother deemed "suitable."

Now, as a result, she knew she had almost zero self-confidence. She felt about as capable as a clam. So she'd been desperately pleased when Marvin had voiced his proposition. Actually, she'd jumped at it.

He didn't seem the controlling type. In fact, he seemed like the typical, rich Beverly Hills husband, who would gladly ignore even a trophy wife if it meant he could have more time for his own pursuits.

Amanda realized Marvin was basically interested in Marvin. His endless rounds of golf, his traveling, his discreet affairs, and attending to his financial business, which practically ran itself. Marvin's father had left him set for life, and Marvin was determined to enjoy it to the hilt.

All she had to do was show up once in a while. And during all that time she didn't have to attend to Marvin, she would have a chance to find herself.

What she wanted, more than anything, was to see what was beyond those estate gates on her own terms. And what she feared, more than anything, was to see what was beyond those estate gates on her own terms.

As a child, it had been all too easy to let her mother make all her decisions. She really hadn't known any better. She'd had no basis for comparison. It had always been just the two of them against the world.

As an adult, her dependence had become a very bad habit, and deeply engrained. She'd rebelled once, in her early teens. Libby had quietly and ruthlessly quashed that youthful uprising. It had never happened again.

Having reached home, Amanda activated the high, wrought-iron gates. They swung open, and she guided the beige Mercedes through them and up the long, circular drive toward the garage. All she could think of was the sanctuary of her room. She needed time away from her mother in order to collect her thoughts.

SAM BEGAN TO PRINT OUT what he'd discovered thus far. Most of the information he'd found on the Internet had been about Libby, including a very impressive Web site complete with recipes and craft tips. There had been surprisingly little about Amanda in any of the articles.

Maybe she doesn't want her devoted public to know how old her only daughter is, Sam thought as he sipped his coffee. *It might reveal her true age.* He smiled as the laser printer came to life and began to spit out pages. *Vanity, thy name is Libby.*

Starting to create these files had taken his mind off Evan, and that had been good. Sam knew he'd been obsessed with finding his partner of seven years. There was still a part of him that couldn't believe Evan had cleaned out the agency's bank account, even though Sam had seen the evidence when he'd gone to the bank.

Finished for the evening, Sam stood, stretched, then walked out from behind his desk and headed toward the comfy chair in front of the television.

The plane's propellers were just about to spin, Rick was just about to send Ilse away, and Sam doubted if he could ever be as selfless as Bogie. In Sam's opinion, finding true love in this world was all too rare.

Hercule whined as Sam picked him up off the chair and settled him in his lap.

"I know. I hate this ending, too. If I loved someone, I don't think I could be this noble."

The bulldog's buggy little eyes remained glued to the screen as Bogie started his desperate speech. As Ingrid Bergman looked up at him, her beautiful face luminous.

And all Sam could think about was Amanda.

SHE COULDN'T SLEEP.

She'd retreated to her room on the third floor as soon as possible. Once she'd changed into her nightgown and robe, she'd wandered down into the spacious kitchen, being very careful not to make a sound, and fixed herself a cup of orange spice tea.

Which she'd finished almost two hours ago. She'd turned off the lights, then slipped into bed and tried to sleep. Rest had eluded her, and she'd tossed and turned, and now found herself out on the balcony outside her bedroom, overlooking the gardens below.

Sam. It always came back to the elusive Sam Cooper.

She would be lying to herself if she didn't admit she'd felt a deep, feminine thrill when he'd taken her into his arms. As if her body had responded to his before her head had had a chance to catch up.

Not your body. Your heart.

She wrinkled her brow as she stared out over the dark garden. *Where did that thought come from?* She didn't have that much experience with giving her heart to anyone. She'd barely even dated, and, at twenty-four, was still a virgin.

My heart... As swiftly as that thought entered her consciousness, she squashed it down, then began to run the silent list through her head that confirmed what she was determined to do.

Marrying Marvin will get me out of the house. Mother will finally leave me alone. I won't have to answer to her concerning every single aspect of my life. Marvin will be gone a great deal of the time.

I might have time to find out exactly who I am....

There was a part of her, deep down inside, that despised her cowardice. Her fear. Countless other young women her age went out and faced the world. Worked jobs, waitressed and sold housewares and books and cosmetics. Did *something* while they figured out what it was they really wanted out of life.

While they waited for their prince.

Amanda took in a deep breath, then let it out in a sigh. She'd long since given up on that idea. Meeting the man of your dreams wasn't the answer. In fact, believing that was part of why it would be so easy for her

to walk down the aisle on Christmas Eve and marry
Marvin. She wasn't sure if she believed in love at all. It
just didn't seem...practical.

She had to be practical because she had to escape.
She'd tried a few times, and been thoroughly defeated.
Humiliated. The last time, just over a year ago, she'd sat
out by the pool and realized how much her mother had
handicapped her. As she had sat there, looking back toward the imposing mansion, Amanda had realized that
she didn't know a single thing about living life outside
her mother's walled estate.

She didn't have a single practical skill.

She could speak several languages fluently, and
knew what each fork was used for in a formal place setting. She knew how to use small talk to make a man feel
at ease. She knew how to listen to him, draw him out,
ask him about his interests and remain quietly at his
side. Smiling, of course.

She knew which wines went with what. What colors
were in fashion. How to apply makeup with the precision of a supermodel.

But she didn't have a clue as to how to interview for a
job, rent an apartment, connect up her own phone, or
even shop at a regular supermarket.

Driving had been a battle. She'd managed to take the
basic course from a private instructor before her mother
had found out, and realized she had an aptitude for it.
She loved to drive, though the beige Mercedes she usually drove was registered in her mother's name.

Libby was nothing if not subtle.

And it wasn't even so much the basic life-skills.
Amanda wasn't stupid. She could have asked Cindy, or
checked a book out of the library. She could have asked

anyone, and bumbled her way through it all, as most twentysomethings had done since the beginning of time.

No, what hampered her was fear. That tiny, insidious voice inside her head that told her she would probably fail. That told her she didn't have a right to a life of her own. That told her she had to make up for all the sacrifices her mother had made in order to raise her to adulthood.

That tiny voice her mother had planted firmly in her head.

Ah, fear. And its wicked sister, guilt. Now there was a powerful word. How much that one simple, human reaction could cause a person to do. Amanda lived with guilt, day in and day out. She was on intimate terms with it. And until this evening, she'd been resigned to it, to what she felt she had to do to make things right. To pay that debt to her mother.

Until this evening. Until Sam Cooper had taken her into his arms and whirled her around the ballroom floor at the Beverly Wilshire Hotel.

Until he had brought feelings to life that had been buried deep within her for a long time. *Forever...*

Amanda closed her eyes and leaned against the balcony railing. With her champagne-colored bathrobe drawn closely around her, the misty, foggy night didn't seem quite as cold. She breathed in the night air, felt the slight chill against her face, and as she hugged her sides, she tried to remember what it had felt like, dancing with Sam.

Her body remembered instantly, and she flushed from head to toe, her eyes opening, her breath a sharp intake against the remembered sensation. Her rational

mind seemed to disappear, only to be replaced by a
yearning so strong it compelled her thoughts in directions she fought against.

What would it be like to kiss him?

She didn't even want to go in that direction.

But she did.... Sam Cooper was a man who would fill
any woman's mind with sexual curiosity, a desire to
know what could happen between them. He was the
sort of man who would be passionate with the woman
he loved, and very direct. A man who would pull her
down on the sheets and make love to her until she was
exhausted. Satiated.

She'd sensed that when she'd danced with him, that
feminine instinct coming into play. Because all the sig-
nals had been there. The intensity in his eyes. The way
he'd touched her. With most men, she wasn't even curious about kissing them, but with Sam...she imagined
it all.

There would be no sleep for her this night. Thoughts
of this man made her feel restless. Incomplete. Filled
with a kind of longing, and she didn't even know why.
It wasn't just sexual, though there were those feelings to
consider. Sam Cooper made her think of emotions she
didn't want to feel, things she couldn't afford to want....

Consciously, Amanda shifted her thoughts. The day
after tomorrow, she had a lunch with Cindy she looked
forward to. Even her mother couldn't censor all her
friends, and though Libby didn't particularly care for
Cindy, she considered her relatively harmless.

Then later the following week, more preparations for
the wedding. Last-minute fittings on the dress her
mother had picked out. Making sure her shoes were
comfortable. Double-checking with the florist and ca-

terers. And with Pierre, the French pastry chef who was in charge of that masterpiece of a wedding cake.

None of it touched her. Libby would be in her glory, making all the arrangements, all the decisions.

None of it touched her, Amanda thought as she slowly walked back inside her dark bedroom. Because she couldn't afford to feel deeply about anything. Or anyone.

Especially Sam Cooper. Wherever he was.

"ALL RIGHT, THIS IS what we're going to do."

Hercule looked up at Sam, an expression of utter trust in his dark, doggy eyes.

Sam sat back in his chair and surveyed the printouts on his desk. Though Amanda Hailey had been elusive, and harder to put together than her celebrity mother, he'd managed to create quite a credible file on her.

Sam always tried to come up with one word that described a potential client and their emotional motivation. One word that would stay in his head and help him understand the person he would have to deal with during his time on the assignment.

This one word, in Amanda Hailey's case, had been criminally easy.

Sheltered.

Her life read like an elegant little leather-bound book of privilege. Private Swiss boarding schools. The right vacations. The correct purchases—clothes, shoes, cars. A life so carefully mapped out, so incredibly orchestrated, that there was no room for a man like himself.

No wonder she'd walked off the dance floor. Sam picked up another sheet of the extensive printout and studied it, then took a swig of his chocolate protein shake. It was an easy breakfast, and one he liked.

"But I felt something between us, you know?"

Hercule whined, then hunched down farther in the sleeping bag and covered his wrinkled little head with his front paws.

"Oh, come on, you're a bigger romantic that I am!" Sam didn't worry about his sanity, talking to the dog. He'd carried on regular discussions with Hercule long before his ex-partner Evan had cleared out the agency's bank account and skipped town. For Sam's money, Hercule was better than a therapist. Cheaper, too.

"The question is, how can I convince her that I'm the man she should marry without scaring the hell out of her? I think she thought I had a screw loose last night."

Hercule whined again, this time from beneath the folds of the sleeping bag.

Sam finished his shake, set the large glass down, then stood and stretched. "Let's go for a walk and blow out the cobwebs."

At the word "walk," Hercule darted out from beneath the sleeping bag and raced for the door, yapping excitedly.

"Walk. Yeah, you understand that one."

The beach was always gorgeous in the early morning, pristine and untouched. As no one was about, Sam let Hercule off the leash, and the bulldog raced for the waves, barking furiously. He knew better than to mess with the seagulls or pelicans, and simply played a game with the white foam as it crashed against the sand.

Sam jogged behind the dog, enjoying the feel of working his muscles. He'd done some stretching exercises earlier. Now he needed the crisp, cool morning air to clear his brain and help him figure out how to proceed.

He was halfway down the beach, following the excited bulldog, when it came to him.

Cindy. The best friend. With more skittish clients, the direct approach never worked. It would be far more productive to come at Amanda from another angle, an angle she wouldn't be expecting. Cindy was good. Cindy, in fact, was excellent. For Cindy, according to what he'd overheard last night on his cell phone, was already partly on his side.

Well, not on *his* side, exactly. But definitely not on Marvin's. And that was just the in he needed.

Cindy Walpert. Amanda's best friend since they'd attended private school together. She'd been identified in a photo with Amanda, and Sam had written down Cindy's last name. After all, how many Cindys could Amanda know?

Cindy had gone with her to Europe, had lived in the same ritzy neighborhood as Amanda with her divorced father, a hotshot executive at one of the major studios. That was probably the reason Libby Hailey had even approved of her daughter's friendship—Cindy was from the right sort of family. Rich.

But from what he'd overheard on his cell phone the other night, Cindy seemed to have survived her wealthy, privileged upbringing with some common sense intact. Sam couldn't see Cindy jumping at the chance to marry a man like Marvin. And she was actively discouraging Amanda.

If I could get to Cindy…talk to her…

Perhaps she still lived at home. Many young women her age did. He would get her father's address from his

extensive collection of CD-ROMS that held names and
addresses throughout the United States. Or perhaps
one of his contacts in Beverly Hills could get him the information if the number was unlisted.

This could actually work.

"Hercule!" he called into the wind, and the small
black bulldog came running back to his side, panting
excitedly, a lone, worn-out child's sneaker dangling
from his jaws. Hercule loved shoes passionately, more
than anything else in the world. Sam had several damaged pairs in his closet that attested to this fact.

He dropped down to his knees and began to wrestle
the athletic shoe from the bulldog.

Stubborn. Hercule was as stubborn as they came.

"Drop it."

Soft growls.

Sam pulled harder on the heel of the shoe. "*Drop* it!"

Louder growls.

Finally, after a humiliatingly long time, he managed
to wrestle the shoe away from an obsessed Hercule,
who then stood panting at his side, flashing him that
doggy grin that seemed to say, "There now, wasn't *that*
a fun time?" Sam snapped the leash back on his canine
friend's collar and led the way home to the now closed
nightclub.

That was one advantage, living above Nick's at
Night. During the day, the place was dead. Quiet as a
tomb. He had all the time in the world to think about
what he was going to do with his life.

Upstairs, he gave Hercule a dog biscuit, then gathered his files together in some sort of order and stuffed
them into a briefcase. They would go with him in the
Miata tomorrow morning, along with several current

paperback bestsellers, a few Books on Tape, some CDs, and a large bottle of water. After, of course, he had ferreted out Cindy's father's address and knew exactly where it was he was going.

Stakeouts were hard work. You had to prepare.

SAM PARKED ACROSS THE street and just slightly beyond Cindy's father's house at eight the next morning. He pulled his baseball cap down low on his face and pretended to be studying a map. One couldn't be too careful these days, what with stalkers, jealous husbands and crazed fans. He didn't want to do anything unscrupulous. He just wanted a chance to talk to Cindy.

He'd tried to dress to look as harmless as possible, in blue jeans and a navy T-shirt, athletic shoes, baseball cap and the requisite dark glasses.

Sam waited. And waited. Then waited some more. He pulled out a Books on Tape adaptation of a detective novel he'd been meaning to get to, and slipped the tape into his Walkman. It amused him, to read mystery and detective novels, and see how the writers embellished what was usually a long and boring job.

At precisely eleven-thirty, the electronic gates to the Walpert estate swung open, and Sam went on the alert. He watched as a vintage black Mustang convertible sped through the gates. And recognized the sleek, dark-haired woman behind the wheel as Cindy Walpert, best friend and sensible sidekick of Amanda Hailey.

"Show time," he muttered as he started his car, put it in gear, then slid out of the unobtrusive parking place and followed the Mustang south, down the lush, palm-tree-lined residential street toward Sunset Boulevard.

3

He followed her into Beverly Hills, parked in the same parking structure, then watched as she walked into a trendy little bistro.

Lunch. Probably with Amanda. Sam had already decided that if Cindy were meeting with a male friend, he would leave her alone. He didn't want to muck up anyone else's love life. But if she was having a casual lunch with the girls, or with Amanda, he would move in for some information.

Once inside the restaurant, he approached the hostess. She smiled up at him, all golden-tanned skin, green eyes and long blond hair. Sam returned the friendly smile.

"Did you just see a woman, brunette, short hair, wearing a tangerine-colored sundress?"

"I just seated her."

"Who is she with?"

"Another woman. A blonde."

Bingo.

"Can you seat me next to them?"

The hostess looked worried. "You're not some jealous-husband type, are you?"

"On my honor, I won't cause any trouble." He lowered his voice for her ears alone. "I'm not even working for a jealous husband. I just have to get some information."

"Are you a detective or something?"

Sam didn't really want to go into detail at this point. "Or something." He handed her a twenty-dollar bill. "I'd really appreciate it."

Money talked. Even though this was Beverly Hills, one of the most monied cities on the planet, he would bet she wasn't making much over minimum wage. Some things never changed.

"Right this way, sir."

AMANDA GLANCED UP FROM studying her menu as the man she had spent all of last night sexually fantasizing about was seated at the table next to her on the sunny, plant-filled patio. She glanced down at the menu again, then back up, and registered the fact that Sam was no more than a few feet away from her. Her face flamed, and she occupied herself with studying a menu she was already familiar with.

If he only knew...

"What's wrong?" Cindy whispered, and Amanda wished, not for the first time, that she had a friend who was a little less perceptive. But then, that friend wouldn't be Cindy.

"It's him," Amanda muttered from behind her menu, trying to use it as a shield so she couldn't see Sam.

"Him?"

"Him. The guy at the reception the other night."

"Oh my God!" A quick look on Cindy's part, then she whispered, "He's good-looking."

"I know."

"*Really* good-looking, Amanda."

"I *know*."

"Don't get mad," Cindy whispered. "I'm just stating

the obvious. Good-looking in a kind of renegade way, like the way Brad Pitt looked in *Legends of the—*"

"Stop."

Amanda could clearly tell that Cindy knew she'd hit a nerve. So her friend returned her attention to her menu, and Amanda prayed for a waiter so they could tell him or her they'd changed their minds and didn't want to have lunch here after all. It was one thing to fantasize about Sam, and quite another to see him in the flesh....

"Ladies?" Their waiter arrived, all slender grace and personality. His dark hair was perfectly cut, his face evenly tanned. Amanda recognized a struggling actor.

"Have we decided what we're going to have?" the waiter asked. He flashed them both a smile, his teeth white and even. "The corn chowder is killer today."

"I think we're going to—" Amanda began.

"Amanda? Is that you?"

She closed her eyes. That *voice*. Dark and smoky, full of sensual promises...

He'd found her.

SAM COULD TELL AMANDA wasn't thrilled. He would have to move fast. He got up quickly and moved to her side.

"Amanda, I thought it was you! What a surprise, seeing you here! And this must be—"

"Cindy." Cindy stuck out her hand, and Sam shook it. "Cindy Walpert."

"Sam Cooper. Nice to meet you. So, are you two having lunch?"

"Are we all having lunch together?" the waiter asked brightly.

"No," said Amanda.

"Yes," said Sam.

"Why not?" said Cindy.

The waiter moved aside and brought another glass of water with the requisite slice of lemon while Sam pulled his chair over to Amanda and Cindy's table and settled in.

"Have you all decided what you'd like to order, or should I give you a few more minutes?"

"Cobb salad for me," Cindy said. "Hold the bacon."

"That sounds good," Sam said. "I'll have the same." He didn't really care what he ate for lunch—his attention was on Amanda. She looked like a frightened deer on a mountain road, facing a pair of bright, oncoming headlights.

"And you?" the waiter asked Amanda.

"I—uh—"

"You like the angel-hair pasta with basil and fresh tomatoes," Cindy suggested. Sam could tell that Cindy knew her friend was upset, but was watching her, curious.

"Fine."

Their waiter departed with their order, and Sam took a long swig of his glass of water. "Nice place," he said, striving for neutral ground. "You two come here often?"

"It's one of our favorites," Cindy volunteered. "You?"

He'd never been inside this restaurant before, but he wasn't about to say so. "A few times. That angel-hair pasta is good, isn't it?"

Dead silence from Amanda.

This wasn't working.

Their waiter returned with a basket filled with hot bread, rolls and breadsticks, along with a small crock containing pats of butter. Trying not to move suddenly and startle Amanda even more, Sam helped himself to a piece of the French bread and buttered it lavishly. It had been a long time since his morning shake.

"So, Sam, what do you do?" Cindy asked.

He knew immediately what she was up to. Protecting her friend. Feeling him out. If he wasn't careful, she would be asking him if his intentions toward Amanda were honorable.

"I have my own business."

"Really." She paused, breadstick in hand, her dark eyes assessing. "Doing what?"

He didn't dare glance at Amanda. "I'm a private investigator."

"Do you like it?"

"It has its moments." He decided to turn the tables on her. "What do you do, Cindy?"

"I'm starting up a mail-order business. I design women's clothing, and I do a lot of painting on silk. One-of-a-kind fabrics, that sort of thing."

"You could do very well, living in this area," he said.

"No kidding. Every season I wonder what the designers were thinking. Sometimes the fashions for women are so ugly."

Sam took a deep, steadying breath. He turned toward Amanda. "And what do you do?"

She glanced down at her hands, and Sam could see those slender fingers shaking. For just a moment, he really disliked himself. He'd wanted to save her, not frighten her. He couldn't bear the thought that she might actually be afraid of him.

He didn't want her to be afraid of him. The thoughts he had about her, the decidedly erotic daydreams he'd imagined had nothing to do with fear.

"Nothing," she said, her voice low. He could barely catch the words. "I don't really do anything."

Silence.

"Oh, Amanda," Cindy said finally. "That's not true."

She didn't answer.

This was going very badly. Sam knew he had to do something. He couldn't stand seeing her in such discomfort.

"Amanda," he said, keeping his voice low. Soothing. "It wasn't my intention to ruin your lunch. I have the feeling you don't really like my being here."

Her cheeks flushed with color again. She seemed almost painfully shy. Sam continued.

"I'm going to leave. But before I do, I have to repeat what I said the other night. I think that marrying Marvin is a really bad idea. I think you'd be doing yourself a lot of damage. You have time to change your mind, and I hope you'll give me a chance." He took one last sip of his water, then slid his chair back from the table.

"It was nice meeting you, Cindy. I'll flag down our waiter on the way out and cancel my salad."

"At least get it to go," Cindy said, and he saw genuine regret in those dark brown eyes. Instinct told him she was on his side.

"I'm leaving you my business card, Amanda," he said, extracting one from his wallet. "You can call me. Any time. Day or night. About anything." He hesitated, then instinct told him to plunge ahead. "I think you have a terrific friend here, but you can always use another. I'd like to be that person."

That got her attention. Amanda stared at him as he placed his business card on the table, got up and left the sunny little restaurant.

SHE DIDN'T KNOW WHAT to say. Amanda couldn't quite meet Cindy's eyes as Sam left the bistro's patio section. In all of her life, she'd never reacted to a man like she'd reacted to Sam. Never thought the things she had, never wanted to explore that wild, reckless side she kept carefully hidden away.

But seeing him in person... He practically paralyzed her, she was so aware of him. She'd never felt these emotions with any other man. Ever. From the instant she'd seen him, she'd felt as if her body wasn't her own. It belonged to another woman, one even less sure of herself than she was.

"He's wonderful," Cindy breathed.

Amanda opened her mouth to contradict her friend, then found she couldn't. There was something really wonderful about Sam. He fascinated her. Where some men might have blundered on through the highly uncomfortable lunch, he'd recognized what was happening, commented on it, and corrected the situation in the only way he'd known how.

Slowly, tentatively, she reached forward and picked up the business card he'd left on the table. It was a light gray, with bold black lettering.

The Blackthorne Agency

Sam Cooper, Private Investigator

Cindy leaned over, staring unabashedly.

"It sounds like something out of a Sam Spade novel!"

Amanda wrinkled her nose. "Or one of your mysteries."

"Or one of your romance novels," Cindy countered.

She had to admit it. "It does sound awfully romantic. Blackthorne. What a wonderful name. I wonder where he got it?"

"Blackthorne," Cindy mused. "It makes me think of an English mansion on a windswept moor. Somewhere in Cornwall, like in a Daphne du Maurier novel."

"Or an old movie. Like Joan Fontaine in *Rebecca*."

"Or Gene Tierney in *Laura*—"

"Or perhaps Ingrid Bergman in *Gaslight*," their waiter interjected as he placed their orders in front of them. "Where did that gentleman go? Someone told the cook to put a hold on that second Cobb salad."

"So he didn't take it to go," Cindy said.

"No. Katie, our hostess, said he walked out looking like a man whose heart had been broken." The waiter smiled down at them, softening his next words. "Girls, it's not even past noon, and you've already broken a man's heart?"

"Not me," Cindy said with a grin, picking up her fork and digging into her salad. "Her."

"My, my," their waiter said. "As my mother used to say, I wouldn't throw him out of bed for eating crackers."

SAM DROVE BACK TO THE beach, then took Hercule for a long walk. He wasn't sure what he was going to do next, but in his line of work, he'd learned that sometimes the only thing a P.I. could do was put out his feelers and wait until something happened.

He'd given her his card. As much as he wanted to pursue her, wanted to be with her, he would have to trust Amanda to make the next move.

"SOMETHING WRONG WITH the pasta?" Cindy commented.

"No, I— I'm just—" Amanda set down her fork. "I'm too upset to eat."

"Why?"

"He— What happened— Sam—"

"Yes?"

"He just upsets me."

"Wonderful!"

"I must have missed something here."

"Amanda, you're wonderfully naive. The reason our Mr. Cooper upsets you is because you're in the process of falling in love with him. Didn't those novels we read throughout boarding school teach you anything?"

"But those are men in books. They don't exist in real life."

"Sometimes they do. And I think our Mr. Cooper is a card-carrying member of that particular club. That guy has testosterone to burn, and then some."

Amanda covered her face with her hands. "You noticed it, too? It's not just me?"

"Oh, my God! That smile! That body! He should be declared a lethal weapon. But, lucky you, he only had eyes for you. Now, the real question is, are you going to take that card? And the next question is, are you going to call him and let him be a friend?"

"Cindy, he wants to be more than my friend." The idea secretly thrilled her.

"No kidding. Are you going to call him?"

Amanda hesitated.

"I would," Cindy said.

"Of course you would. You're not afraid of anything."

"I have my moments. Amanda, are you going to call him?"

"If I call him—" She hesitated, then forced the next words out. "If I call him, I think I'll end up not marrying Marvin."

"Then that would be reason enough!"

"You don't understand, Cindy. It's more complicated than that."

"Don't start with that business about how much you owe your mother, because I'm not buying it."

"But I do. She sacrificed a lot for me, and—"

"Not enough that she deserves the rest of your life. You don't have to pay that kind of price."

"But the marriage wouldn't be—"

"A real marriage. I know. Forget it, Amanda. This is no marriage of convenience. At least in the books, she gets to look at and live with a gorgeous man. You get Marvin. Uh-uh. No way. I can't even pretend to think this is a good idea."

"Cindy, I—"

"Take that card. That's it, pick it up. Now slide it into your purse, and tonight when your mother's busy arranging dried flowers or trying out a new recipe for a party dip, I want you to call this man and—"

But she couldn't. She knew she couldn't. Sam Cooper was the sort of man who would change a woman's life forever. Though she had thought of him constantly, Amanda wasn't sure she was ready to take that first step.

Calmly, pushing down the mixture of intense emotions that seemed to be boiling inside her, Amanda ripped the gray business card in half and placed it in the glass ashtray.

Cindy stared, astounded. "You're not even going to give him a chance?"

Amanda stared at the two halves of the ripped card. Until the moment she'd torn it in half, she hadn't known it was possible to feel so utterly dejected. So forlorn. Like she'd lost something crucial before she'd even had a chance to experience it. But she had to do it. Any other course of action would be impossible. Unwise. Imprudent.

Any other course of action would risk throwing caution completely to the wind.

"No." There was a finality to the way she said the words, and Cindy must have heard it because she calmly picked up her fork and began to finish her salad.

"I DON'T THINK SHE'S going to call," Sam said, after picking up the remote and pausing the video of *To Have and Have Not*.

From beneath the sleeping bag strewn across the comfortable leather couch, Hercule the bulldog whined.

"Oh, give me some support, you coward! Lie a little!"

Hercule jumped into his lap and gave Sam's stubbly jaw a quick swipe with his pink tongue.

"That's better." Sam studied Bogart's frozen image on the television screen. "Now this guy, he would have kidnapped her from the restaurant and simply brought her home. Held her captive until she finally realized she'd fallen in love with him."

Hercule barked his approval—once, twice. He loved Humphrey Bogart.

"Ah, but she's been held captive all her life. I just couldn't do it."

Hercule whined, then pawed the remote control.

"Maybe you're right. A little more distraction is in order. And if that doesn't work, there's always the Häagen-Dazs in the fridge."

Hercule barked again. He knew that word, and he loved ice cream.

Sam pressed the Play button, and settled in for some serious viewing.

STANDING NEAR THE CASH register out front, Cindy studied the change in her hand and came to an abrupt decision.

"Hang on, Amanda, I want to go give him another dollar. I didn't have enough change before."

"Sure. I'll wait here."

Cindy turned, change in hand, and started back toward their table out on the plant-filled patio area. As she came through the door, she saw their waiter cautiously fishing the two pieces of Sam Cooper's business card out of the ashtray.

"Drop that or you're a dead man."

He sighed. "You can't blame a guy for trying."

"I know. I would've done the same, if they weren't utterly and completely perfect for each other."

"What's the problem?" he asked, pretending to wipe down their table once again.

"Her mother. The woman makes Leona Helmsley look like an amateur."

He raised his eyebrows. "The queen of mean?"

"And then some." She looked up at him. "Just what were you planning to do with this card?"

"Honey, I was going to call him and ask him if I could pay him to do a little investigating for me."

Cindy couldn't help but laugh. "That's very good. You know, you're wasted as a waiter. Has anyone told you that you should be performing?"

"All the time. It's getting them to sign that paycheck that's rough."

"ALL SET?" AMANDA asked as Cindy returned.

"Yep."

They walked out of the restaurant together, the two halves of Sam's business card tucked safely inside Cindy's purse.

Sometimes, Cindy thought as she walked to her car, *love needs just a little help. And I'm just the person to do it.*

SAM WAS ON HIS SECOND bowl of Ben & Jerry's Chunky Monkey, and had already picked out all the semisweet chocolate chunks, when the phone rang. He was so despondent he let the answering machine pick up.

"The Blackthorne Agency wants to help you, but we're all out on stakeouts, so if you'll leave your name and number, we'll get back to you within twenty-four hours—"

Beep!

"Sam? Sam, pick up, I know you're there! It's me, Cindy, from lunch today! Damn it, Sam, I know you're—"

He practically killed Hercule, dropping his ice cream and scrambling over the couch to get to the phone on his big, battered walnut desk.

"Cindy! Hey, good to hear from you!" This was a stroke of luck he hadn't dreamed of. Maybe Amanda didn't want to talk to him just yet, but her friend did.

Excellent.

"Look, I'll make it brief. Amanda tore up your card and threw it in the ashtray—"

Sam closed his eyes. He was surprised how much that hurt.

"But don't get your boxers in a twist, because she told me herself that she couldn't possibly call you because if she called you she didn't think she could possibly marry Marvin and that would be unthinkable because of all that she owes her mother."

Sam considered all this. "You have incredible breath control, Cindy. That was an amazing sentence."

"Well, I'm one of eleven. Lots of step-siblings. My father's married four different times and let me tell you, the guy was fruitful. He's in his early sixties, and his current wife had twin boys just a few years ago."

"That's impressive."

"Yeah, well, he takes care of all of us and somehow makes it work. Anyway, I was somewhere in the middle and I had to learn to talk and eat fast or I never would have survived. Did you get all that?"

"Amanda tossed my card. She can't call me. She calls me, Marvin's history. And Marvin being history makes Mommy Dearest mad as hell."

"God, you're quick. I like smart men."

He laughed, then got down to work. "Are you willing to answer a few questions?"

"Ask me and I'll tell you."

"What's in it for Libby Hailey?" Sam smiled as he

heard Cindy sound as if she'd thrown back her head and laughed.

"Got it in one. That woman doesn't get out of bed if there's not something in it for her. I've been asking myself the same question since this whole wedding scheme was cooked up. Marvin has a ton of money, that's all I know."

"Is some of that cash finding its way back to Libby?"

"You mean, is she selling her daughter's hand in marriage? God, that sounds pretty sordid, doesn't it?"

"The truth often is."

"I wouldn't put anything past her. But Sam, before this goes any further, I have a question for you."

"Shoot."

"It's kind of personal, and pretty early in the game, and I know it may sound insane, but—"

"Go for it."

"Do you love her? And I don't mean just love her, I mean love her the way Bogie loved Bacall, the way Olivier loved Vivien Leigh, the way Cary Grant loved Grace Kelly in—"

Sam smiled. This woman spoke his language.

"*To Catch a Thief*," he said. "Or the way he fell in love with Leslie Caron in—"

"*Father Goose*," Cindy finished for him. "Do you love her that way? Because if you don't, get lost. Now. She's had her heart torn apart way too many times already, and she's only twenty-four—"

"I love her." He could hear Cindy letting out her breath in a long, tension-releasing sigh. "I don't know why or how, but I want to see where this can go. Because I think she's the one."

"Good. Oh, thank God. I thought you were the one

when I saw you today, but I had to be sure before this conversation went any further. Can you come over for dinner tonight? Alice is fixing chicken and dumplings."

"Sure." He didn't know what Cindy was up to, but he had a feeling it would help his cause.

"Great. We'll eat early, around six." She gave him her address, which he already knew. "Afterward, there are some things I want to show you."

"I'll be there." Sam hung up the phone, then returned to a sparkling clean bowl devoid of any ice cream, and a guilty-looking Hercule peeking from beneath the covers. But Sam felt so good, he didn't have the heart to punish him.

SAM RETRACED HIS STEPS back to Beverly Hills, to Cindy's father's mansion high in the hills. Only this time, he got to drive the black Miata through the iron gates and into the driveway.

Cindy answered the door, still dressed in the tangerine sundress, but with a pale yellow cardigan thrown on over it. The colors should have clashed, but on Cindy they looked stunning.

Dinner was a lively affair. Two of Cindy's brothers were there, one a film student at USC, the other taking screenwriting classes at UCLA. Her stepmother and the twin boys were also at dinner, and the conversation was fast and furious.

Afterward, he and Cindy retired to the library, a huge room lined with books. A wide-screen television dominated one corner of the room. Cindy settled Sam in one of the comfortable chairs, offered him an after-dinner cup of excellent coffee, then began to rummage through a huge collection of videos.

He refrained from asking her what she was up to. All in good time. Instead, he enjoyed the quiet, the delicious coffee, the sense of relaxation. Sam had a feeling that Cindy had grown up in a very different kind of family from Amanda's. And that she had been a godsend to the lonely girl Amanda must have been, and probably still was.

"Got it," Cindy muttered, then stood and approached the television. She turned on the entertainment center, then slipped the tape into one of several VCRs flanking the huge TV.

"Just watch this for a moment, and then I'll explain."

The lights dimmed, and a tape began. It took Sam a moment before he realized he was watching a collection of commercials, most of them very familiar.

In the first one, an adorable blond toddler ran along the beach. Her mother, a stunning model, picked her up and held her close as a bottle of expensive perfume was advertised.

In another, the same little girl promoted suntan lotion. In another, she smiled as she ate cereal. Then a slightly older blond girl held a doll as she sat beneath a sparkling Christmas tree. Clearly a holiday commercial.

He watched commercial after commercial for almost thirty-five minutes before Cindy's voice in the darkened library brought him out of the moment.

"Seen enough?"

He'd already guessed. "Amanda?"

"Yep. You know, she made thousands before she reached the age of ten. And I'd guess she still doesn't have her own bank account."

Sam swore softly. He'd had no idea.

"Her mother has this—this *thing* about money.

There's never enough. Never. It's like a sickness. I mean, my dad makes a lot of money, but it's not the same."

"I know what you mean," Sam said, still thinking over what he'd seen on the screen. He knew, from his information gathering, that she'd done television work, but seeing it was different. That blond toddler had possessed an almost wistful quality. Had held on to that model-perfect mother on the beach with the small arms of a child who desperately wanted to be held. Loved. He'd sized Libby up from the moment he'd met her at the Beverly Wilshire, and had rightly pegged her as a cold, cold woman.

When he'd seen that little girl on the videotape, his eyes had stung. Because he'd seen deeper than the commercial, to the emotional child who hadn't been acting. That emotion had come across on camera, and had probably sold millions of bottles of perfume.

"She sold her daughter long before this damn wedding," Sam muttered. He could feel the anger rising in him, a fine, humming sensation that heightened every nerve ending. No matter what happened between him and Amanda, Sam knew he couldn't let her marry that old man.

"Sam," Cindy said as she sat down across from him in another comfortable chair. "Sam, I met Amanda when she was twelve years old. We went to the same boarding school. She was so painfully shy, I can't tell you. The other girls thought she was stuck-up because of all the television work. They made her life a living hell."

"But you didn't."

"Nope. All I had at home was brothers, and I'd always wanted a sister. Always. No one else would room with her but me. She didn't talk to me for almost six weeks, but I finally broke through that wall, that reserve—"

He could imagine it. If anyone could have taken down those bricks Amanda had firmly mortared into place, it would have been Cindy.

"She's one of the finest people I've ever met, and she doesn't deserve what's happened to her. And what's about to happen, if we don't stop it."

"She's never tried to get away?"

"Libby is her *mother.* Who could see this objectively? I'd be into a little denial myself. You've got to understand, Amanda has always been the good girl. She's been pleasing her mother since she could walk, doing whatever she told her. Or whatever whichever director she worked with said."

Sam slowly nodded his head. He could understand now. How could Amanda know anything different, when the carefully controlled life her mother had laid out for her was all she'd ever experienced?

"Sam, I've been trying to get her to back out of this wedding since I first heard about it."

"Me, too." Briefly he told Cindy about overhearing their conversation on his cellular phone the night of the reception.

"It's fate." She sat back and looked at him, delighted. "It was fate that Amanda and I met at that boarding school, and it's fate that you stepped into the picture right before the wedding. I couldn't do it alone. But the moment I saw the two of you together this afternoon, I knew that between the two of us, we could stop this wedding."

"Why do you say that?" If there was one thing Sam had learned in his line of work, it was to always, always, *always* trust a woman's intuition.

"The way she looked. As if she'd just been hit by a truck."

"How flattering."

"You know what I mean! And, the fact that she said, and I quote, 'If I call him, I won't marry Marvin.' You see, Sam, a woman *knows* these things."

He nodded his head. "How do you think we should go about this?"

"I think you have to wear down her resistance through constant exposure. You've got to show up wherever she goes. Everywhere. Movies, shopping, classes, the country club—"

"I draw the line at salons."

"I won't make you get your legs waxed, Sam. No pedicures. And I won't make you get dressed up in women's clothing, though it worked for Cary Grant. But if you had to—"

"I would."

"Good."

Sam jumped in. "You let me know where she's going, and I'll be there. I'll give you my beeper number, and you give me yours. Mine has voice mail—just give me the time and the place, and I'll show up."

"Great." She reached for one of his hands, held it tightly, then closed her eyes. "Sam, this has to work."

He patted her hand, touched beyond measure at the depth and strength of her friendship with Amanda. The image of that blond toddler reaching for the imaginary mother who loved and wanted her tore at his heart.

"It will. It will."

4

SAM WAS IN THE MIDDLE of a very interesting dream that involved himself, Amanda, and their two very naked bodies, when he heard bells ringing. Strange. In these sorts of dreams, he usually wasn't interrupted—

"The Blackthorne Agency wants to help you, but we're all out on stakeouts, so if you'll leave your name and number, we'll get back to you within twenty-four hours—"

Beep!

"Sam, it's about five-thirty. This is Cindy. This evening, the Beverly Center, the theaters at the top floor of the shopping center. Be there! Amanda and I are going to a seven-thirty showing of—"

Sam stumbled his way from the black leather couch he and Hercule had been sprawled out on, napping. Sam had been up until almost six in the morning, checking out lead after lead on his partner, Evan. Reading all his E-mail posted by various contacts throughout the world. Leaving them messages. Trying to find the skunk. Because if he could find this particular skunk and vindicate the agency, he might have a prayer of possibly taking on some cases besides those of the lost-poodle variety.

"Hello."

"Sam, you're there. Thank God. I'm meeting Amanda for a movie at the Beverly Center tonight, I wanted you to know. I'm going to try and time it so that we'll be in line right about seven. Follow us, and wait until we buy our tickets."

"Good thinking," he said. "That way, she can't pick a different movie from the one I'm planning on seeing."

"Right. She's not one to ever make a fuss, so she won't change her mind after we buy our tickets."

"I'll be there."

THE BEVERLY CENTER loomed out of the fog, an imposing, multistoried shopping center trimmed with bright neon. Sam had read somewhere that it had been modeled after a similar shopping center in Paris. Right in the heart of the city, it sheltered many trendy shops, along with an enormous food court and a multiplex movie theater.

He took a ticket as he entered the mammoth parking structure, then found a parking space for the Miata after an arduous search and made his way up several escalators to the top floor, where the movie theater was located.

The entire shopping center had been decorated for Christmas. A huge, sparkling tree graced the main courtyard, numerous intricately wrapped presents beneath its branches. Stores were festooned with ribbons, ornaments, lights and smaller versions of the huge tree. Signs outside the various shops announced great gift ideas—values on clothing, electronic toys, books, CDs, beauty products and cookware.

The escalators were crowded with people, out doing their Christmas shopping during the last few weeks before the holiday. Instead of finding the shopping center overwhelming and the energy tense, Sam enjoyed it. He normally liked the holidays. It just seemed that this Christmas, he had a lot on his mind.

He spotted Amanda's golden hair immediately, beneath the bright lights of the marquee as she and Cindy stood in line. Situating himself so he was concealed by several of the outdoor tables at a small coffee house nearby, Sam waited until the women bought their tickets. The line wasn't too long as it was a Wednesday night. Clearly, more people were interested in their Christmas shopping than a movie.

He watched the transaction, then swiftly walked toward the multiplex and got into line. The theater was brightly lit, with enormous posters gracing the walls of the main lobby, announcing current and coming attractions. The smell of freshly popped popcorn drifted out into the main lobby.

When he was within two people of the cashier, he heard Cindy's voice above the subtle buzzing of the crowd.

"Sam! What are you doing here?"

He turned. "Hey! The same as you, taking in a movie."

"Oh! What are you going to see? Amanda and I just bought tickets for that new French film, *Les Deux Enfants*."

"What a coincidence! That's the film I'd picked out to see tonight." He could see Amanda hovering behind her friend, looking anxious and none too pleased.

"Then join us. We'll wait for you."

He reached the cashier, muttered "the French one," and bought his ticket with a sense of impending doom. Then he remembered that he was willing to do anything—short of murder—to be near Amanda. Anything to make her realize she was throwing her life away on a guy like Marvin.

Sam had a sneaking suspicion that Marvin loved these French films. His own taste leaned more toward action-adventure movies with a hero, a villain and lots of explosions. If there weren't any major explosions during the first fifteen minutes, Sam didn't really consider it to be a real movie.

Of course, his *real* passion was Hollywood's older films. Bogart and Bacall, Tracy and Hepburn, Carole Lombard, Gary Cooper, Jimmy Stewart—the list was endless. But the studios today certainly didn't make them like they used to, or he would have been at the multiplexes every weekend.

He swiftly bought a large popcorn and a Coke, then followed Amanda and Cindy down the hallway to the theater where the foreign film was to be shown. It wasn't much bigger than a private screening room, with nine rows of six seats each, flanking a center aisle. He could have been in someone's living room, except for the enormous screen that dominated the front wall.

"Not one of the more popular selections, I see," he muttered to no one in particular, then made his way down the aisle, following Amanda and Cindy's lead.

"How about right here?" Cindy suggested. Sam noticed that Amanda was making absolutely no suggestions as to what they should do.

"Fine with me."

"Sam, let's put you in the middle because you're the tallest," Cindy said, eyeing a woman dressed entirely in black with an extremely bizarre, full hairstyle and black metallic nail polish. She sat in front of the seat Sam would be occupying, and the limited number of seats in the small theater were filling up fast.

"Fine." Anything that would get him close to Amanda.

She entered first, then sat down. Sam followed, sitting behind the woman with the bizarre, avant-garde hairstyle. Then Cindy followed, taking the aisle seat.

Within minutes, the lights dimmed and the previews of coming attractions began, with state-of-the-art sound blasting through the small theater and practically vibrating the seats.

Sam could feel the tension emanating from Amanda as he sat next to her. He decided to scrap his original plan of stretching his arm out and trying to ease it around her shoulders. He couldn't move that fast, or he would really scare her away.

What he had to do, as soon as possible, was figure out why she was so...*nervous* around him. *Nervous* wasn't quite the right word, but it was the best he could come up with at the moment.

He'd thought about this a lot while he'd been calling up his E-mail, phoning various leads, and trying to locate Evan. He'd also been working on adding to his master file on Amanda.

The Swiss boarding school clearly hadn't helped her sense of self. At an all-girl establishment, she couldn't have had the normal experiences American high-school students usually had in their four years of education. Amanda probably didn't have a clue about the opposite sex. Sam wondered if she'd ever even been on a real date. She didn't seem to possess the innate confidence of a young woman who had gone out a lot.

Though Cindy had attended the same boarding

school, she'd had her large and boisterous family, mostly male, to give her some perspective on men. Sam also suspected that Cindy's father cared about her a lot more than Amanda's mother did.

As he thought about all this, more previews flashed across the huge screen, the sound blaring. Sam brought his hand up to his mouth, trying to conceal a yawn. He wondered if he shouldn't have bought a double espresso instead of the large tub of popcorn.

He'd just settled down for his nap when Cindy had called, so all in all, he'd gotten barely an hour of real sleep last night. And most of that had involved some extremely erotic, restless dreaming. Half enviously, he thought of Hercule, probably at this moment snoozing contentedly beneath the sleeping bag on the couch.

Now, the thought of sitting through a two-and-a-half-hour French epic—he'd asked the guy who'd sold him his popcorn how long the film ran—with as little sleep as he'd gotten last night seemed a unique form of torture. He wanted Amanda to see him as the type of man who was suave and urbane. Instead, he would probably fall asleep before the opening credits rolled. And snore.

Or worse, drool.

Blinking his gritty eyes, Sam stared at the screen with total concentration and determination. With any luck, it would be a film about the war. World War II, to be exact. If there was any sort of real conflict or drama, he would be all right. Perhaps he would even be blessed with a few explosions. The noise level alone, from these excellent speakers, would shake him right out of his seat.

Or perhaps the film would contain a romance. The

French really knew how to put passion on the screen. And that might get Amanda's subconscious moving in the right direction.

The opening scene, with two French schoolboys pedaling down an idyllic country road on their bicycles and an actor's voice gently telling the beginning of the story in a voice-over, didn't bode well for the rest of the evening.

Stifling a sigh of resignation, Sam took a long swallow of his Coke. He had a feeling he would need all the caffeine he could get.

SHE WAS TOTALLY AWARE of him sitting next to her—with every muscle, every nerve in her body.

Amanda had long ago given up on her white paper bag with two decadently expensive dark chocolate truffles inside. She'd bought them at a candy store in the food court before they'd entered the theater, but now her mind wasn't on chocolate. All she could think of was the man sitting next to her, mere inches away. His presence almost made her sick to her stomach, her heart was racing so fast.

She didn't believe in destiny. She didn't believe in love. She'd long ago given up hoping that things could be different for her. She knew what she had to do.

Then why had fate thrown this man in her path in the first place? And why did he keep showing up everywhere she went? First, the Beverly Wilshire Hotel on the night of her engagement party. Then, at the bistro, while having lunch with Cindy. And now, this evening, at the movies.

She had a swift, disloyal thought about her friend, Cindy, then squelched it. Cindy hadn't even met Sam before, so how could she have told him about her engagement party or their lunch? And why would she? Though Amanda knew her friend didn't want her to marry Marvin, she didn't think Cindy would stoop to stopping the wedding.

Well, Sam Cooper was a P.I. A detective. He could easily have been tailing her. She couldn't see trying to accuse him of stalking her, because he was just too...*nice*.

Nice wasn't the right word, though. "Nice" had nothing to do with the way he made her feel. *Nice* was a word one reserved for tea at four, or Persian kittens, or the feel of a roaring fire after a day of skiing. But "nice" had nothing to do with Sam Cooper.

She didn't feel nice around him. In her dreams, the things they'd done together wouldn't have been considered nice; they would have been called blatantly erotic. And romantic. He brought up all sorts of feelings from deep inside her, feelings she didn't want to experience. Feelings she wanted to keep buried.

Feelings, she had learned at a very early age, were too complicated. Too painful. She'd pushed them away most of her life, and she didn't want to change things now.

She couldn't keep her mind on the story, even though this was a movie she'd been looking forward to for weeks. Both she and Cindy spoke French fluently, and adored foreign films.

Amanda glanced at Sam as he watched the movie. He was blinking his eyes rapidly, and she switched her attention to what was happening on the screen. A chubby, round-faced Frenchwoman was making an

elaborate apple tart, talking to one of the little boys the
entire time, making him laugh.

She had no idea where they were in the story. And
she had no idea what this man was doing in her life. But
she had a very strong feeling that, if she didn't take
swift and preventative action, he was going to turn her
carefully structured world upside down.

MAMAN WAS MAKING an apple tart, smiling as she
talked to her son, offering him her hard-won advice.

Everyone in the theater was watching the foreign film
with rapt attention.

And Sam was fighting a losing battle.

His eyes drifted shut. He just needed to close them
for a moment, ease that gritty, burning feel. If only he
and Hercule had been able to nap for just an hour or
two...

The soft sounds of French seemed to buzz inside his
head. He felt the muscles in his neck ease, then his head
fell back, impossibly heavy, and rested against the
plush back of the theater seat. Then he was drifting,
drifting, drifting—

Until he felt a sharp, insistent jab to his ribs from his
right.

Cindy.

"Sam?" she whispered. "I have to go to the bathroom. I'll be right back."

He didn't even question why she'd told him. He simply silently blessed her for waking him up. He blinked,
reached for his Coke, took another long swallow to
clear his head, and directed his attention toward the
screen.

A wizened old man, complete with a beret, was fixing

one of the boys' bicycles. As he talked, he was apparently imparting some of his hard-won wisdom to the lad.

To Sam, as tired as he was, the actor could have been mouthing his dialogue in Swahili. He blinked again, fighting a losing battle.

What a great way to impress Amanda. Fall asleep in the middle of a movie and prove to her you have the intelligence and sensitivity of a...of a...

He glanced at the screen, saw the two young boys running through a field, the endless voice-over droning on in the background. A black-and-white cow raised its head and glanced at the two children, its body gilded by the golden late-afternoon sunlight.

...of a cow.

Cindy slid into the seat next to him, and he immediately smelled coffee.

"Sam, here's that double espresso you ordered."

He took the cup out of her hand, silently blessing her. The concentrated coffee, when it hit his stomach, was hot and strong, and seemed to sizzle along his nerve endings, bringing him out of his exhausted stupor.

You will get through this... You will get through this.... You will not fall asleep....

He gave his watch a surreptitious glance. Another forty-five minutes to go. Slowly, carefully, Sam took a deep breath. He'd read a study somewhere that had said most yawns were the brain's way of compensating for not enough oxygen. Another breath, slow and steady. Then another slow sip of his espresso.

The film was gradually leached of all color, becoming a grainy black-and-white, and Sam realized this had to be a flashback. Tanks rolled over the country roads, and in the distance, the ground rumbled as something exploded.

He considered this a good omen as he sat back in his seat and proceeded to watch the rest of the film.

AFTER THE MOVIE, Cindy, bless her, suggested they go out for coffee. Sam had the feeling that, after all the caffeine he'd imbibed, he was in for another sleepless night. But that was all right. Just sitting at a small table in the coffeehouse and being able to look at Amanda, made the evening a success.

"So," Sam said, deliberately directing his question toward Amanda, "what did you think of the film?"

She hesitated for a long moment, and Sam didn't rush to fill in the silence. One way or another, he was determined to have a dialogue with this woman. And if she told him she wanted him out of her life, to simply leave her alone, well, he would respect her wishes—until the next time he could arrange another "accidental" meeting.

The waiter placed three coffees in front of them, then glided off.

Silence.

Finally, Cindy broke in. "I thought it was a brilliant evocation of a childhood that was lost. You know, innocence surrendered, that sort of thing."

Sam felt like a high-school English teacher, and Cindy was his star pupil.

Silence.

"Did you like it?" Cindy asked him.

Sam was worried. This was turning into more of a date with Cindy than Amanda. He didn't know how to make her talk to him or even relate to him. He didn't know what to do.

"Yes, I did." He searched his mind frantically, trying not to tell too big a lie. "Especially the flashbacks to the war. I'm a great World War II buff."

Still no response from Amanda.

He decided to go for broke.

"Also, I don't consider a movie to be a movie unless there's at least one good solid explosion, so *Les Deux Enfants* filled the bill." He watched Amanda closely, and was rewarded by the sight of her lips twitching in what he sensed was a smile she was trying to repress.

Maybe she wasn't all that cool and aloof. Maybe she was only shy and inexperienced around men like him. The thought cheered him, as it basically reassured him he was still in the running.

"You know, my brother's the same way!" Cindy said. "No explosions or high-tech gadgetry, and he's bored silly."

"It's that pesky Y chromosome," Sam explained. "It predisposes us to like very loud noises and gadgets."

He was rewarded by the sight of Amanda looking away in order to hide her smile. Instinct told him not to address her, but to simply let her observe him. Over time and continual exposure, she would realize he meant her no harm.

"That scene with the apple tart," Cindy continued. "What do you think that was all about?"

"Well," Sam replied, warming to the topic and all the while watching Amanda out of the corner of his eye, sensing her presence, "it was certainly a visual feast for the eye."

"It was that," Cindy agreed. "I don't even like to

cook, and I was thinking of stopping by Brentano's and picking up a cookbook on French pastry.''

"You could borrow one from my friend, Nick," Sam said.

"Nick?"

"Nick Mangione."

"You know Nick Mangione? The guy who runs Nick's at Night?"

Sam nodded.

"Oh, my God! I saw a special on him on the Food Channel one evening. He's an incredible chef."

"And he knows a thing or two about jazz."

"How did the two of you meet?"

Sam took a breath. Took a plunge. "I don't really want to talk about that now. I feel as if we're leaving Amanda out of the conversation."

There. He'd finally said it. She would have to respond.

And she finally did.

"No, I don't feel left out at all. In fact, I'm...I'm really enjoying myself."

Her voice was soft. Breathy, as if she were having trouble taking a deep breath. As if she were nervous. And Sam was suddenly sure that Miss Amanda Hailey wasn't as calm, cool and collected as she appeared. She had the presence of a young Grace Kelly, all icy and aloof, but he sensed something warmer beneath that surface.

And responded to it.

"All right." He settled back in his chair, eyeing both women, his third espresso in his hands. "Nick and I go way back. I guess it is kind of funny, the way we met. It was a hot day in August, down in Mexico, and Nick was in a bit of a jam...."

SHE LIKED HIM. She really, really liked him.

But she couldn't afford to. Because Sam Cooper could be an incredible complication in her life. Her safe, secure life. The only life she'd ever known.

Amanda remained silent as Cindy drove them back toward Beverly Hills from the shopping center. Los Angeles was once again shrouded in fog, causing the traffic lights and other cars' headlights to loom out of the gray mist and shimmer softly.

She waited for Cindy to say something, to make some sort of comment as she drove down Sunset Boulevard.

But Cindy said nothing.

Amanda didn't encourage any conversation. How could she, when her own thoughts were still so unsettled?

Her friend pulled her black Mustang convertible up to the gated entry of Libby's mansion, then keyed in the code that allowed the imposing wrought-iron gates to swing slowly open. The Mustang climbed the rise up to the circular driveway that flanked the front of the estate.

"Amanda, I need to ask you something," Cindy said.

Here it comes.

"Are you busy tomorrow?"

It wasn't the question Amanda had been expecting.

"No. Why?"

"I still have to get two of my brothers their Christmas presents. I was going to drive down the coast to this huge computer store, and I'd really like some company.

I know that it's right before your wedding, and you probably don't have time—"

Amanda laid a hand on her friend's arm, and Cindy stopped her nervous babbling. "I always have time for you. And it isn't as if I'm really doing anything. Mother is handling it all."

"Can you get away for part of the day?"

"I'm sure I can."

"Fantastic! I'll pick you up at nine."

"I'll be here."

ON THE WAY BACK TO her father's house, Cindy dialed Sam's cellular phone.

"Hey, Sam, it's me. Fry's Electronics, Manhattan Beach, tomorrow right around ten. We'll be in the personal computer section. Oh, and if you could help me pick out something for my brothers, I'd really appreciate it."

"WHY SO FAR AWAY?" Amanda asked the following morning. A strong wind had blown in the night before. The Los Angeles skyline was crystal clear, the sky a bright blue, and the temperature deliciously mild, considering most of the country was blanketed in snow.

Now, sitting in Cindy's convertible as they drove down the coast toward Manhattan Beach and the computer store, she felt free and...happy.

"The prices are unbelievable. Rock bottom. I figure if my brothers want toys for Christmas, I'll get them toys. But the adult-male variety."

Amanda settled back in her seat and enjoyed the sensation of the wind on her face. Somehow, out of her mother's house, in the car with Cindy, she always felt a little more free.

SHE SAW HIM THE INSTANT they entered the store.

Sam, dressed in faded jeans and a Hawaiian shirt in shades of turquoise and peach. Athletic shoes and a baseball cap completed the look. He was talking animatedly with one of the salesclerks.

"Sam?" Cindy said, approaching him.

Amanda, surprised that this time she wasn't quite as annoyed, followed her friend.

"Hey! What are you two doing here?"

"Buying presents for my brothers. Amanda came along to help me pick them out."

"So, you're a computer whiz," he said, directing the question to her.

Amanda swallowed, then said, "I know absolutely nothing about computers. I'm simply here for moral support." She hesitated. "I suppose you know a lot about them?"

"I do."

"Great!" Cindy said. "Then you can help us."

"I'd be delighted."

CINDY SETTLED ON A state-of-the-art fax machine with all the trimmings for her one brother, and an elaborate laptop for the other, along with several software programs for each of them. Sam was quite impressed with the bill, but Cindy simply whipped out her American Express Gold Card and paid for everything on the spot, without even the smallest wince.

"My family makes a really big deal over Christmas," she said as she signed the receipt and handed it back to the dazzled clerk. "It's a lot of fun, with as many people as we have at home."

"What about you?" Sam asked Amanda.

She hesitated. She didn't want to admit to him that she'd spent a lot of Christmas Days over at Cindy's house. There had always been presents for her beneath their tree, and she'd been treated like family.

In sharp contrast, she and her mother usually opened their gifts on Christmas Eve, in front of a roaring fire in the library. Small, discreet, careful gifts. Proper gifts. Usually jewelry, or an item of clothing from an exclusive boutique in Beverly Hills. Nothing that reflected the personality of the gift giver, or the recipient.

The only people Amanda had really loved shopping for gifts for were Cindy and the housekeeper, Maria. With both of them, she'd taken care to match the present to the character of the receiver. She herself had received so much joy from their expressions of happiness as they'd examined their gifts.

"It's a little quieter at home" was all she would admit.

A LITTLE QUIETER...

Sam was sure that statement was true. A little quieter, and probably a whole lot less fun. He had a feeling that Libby Hailey was the sort of mother who whipped up a dazzling feast on Christmas Day for her business associates. For anyone who she thought might help her get ahead in life. But when it came to her only daughter, she relegated her to a place far less important in her life.

He would never be guilty of that.

He took the two women to a little restaurant by the ocean that served excellent seafood. They sat and ate lunch, talked and laughed, then Cindy threw him a fast-ball he almost wasn't prepared for.

"Amanda, I have to go pick up one last present down at a little boutique in Laguna. It's an awfully long drive for you, and I know you only promised me part of the day. Sam, would I be imposing on you if I asked you to drive her back up to Beverly Hills so she doesn't have to spend the rest of the day with me in the car?"

He'd opened his mouth to reply, when Amanda spoke and floored them both.

"I know what you're both up to," she said.

He remained perfectly still, not moving a muscle. And wondered if she'd caught on to the fact that Cindy was telling him her every move, letting him know exactly where they were going to be.

"Cindy, I know you want me to spend some time alone with Sam."

Sam didn't dare meet Cindy's eyes, he was so relieved.

"And Sam, I'm assuming you want to spend some time alone with me."

He cleared his throat. "Yes."

"That's okay, then." She turned in her seat, faced him directly. "Whenever you're ready."

HE'D JUST BEEN HANDED his heart's desire, and now he was nervous.

"What did you have planned for the rest of the day?" he asked, attempting to be heard over the rush of wind and the noise from the other cars on the freeway. Amanda sat in the passenger seat of the Miata as if she'd been born there. He liked the way he felt driving, with her at his side.

"I was going to answer some of my mother's fan mail, but I can do that later."

He liked the fact that she was shuffling her schedule around so they could have time together, and decided to go for broke. "Would you mind if I stopped home just long enough to take my dog out and give him a little bit of a run."

"You have a dog?" She sounded surprised.

"Yes, I do. I also have a mother and father, four sisters and a brother."

There was a short silence. He glanced at her and saw the delicate wash of pink on her high cheekbones.

"I didn't mean it like that."

"I know you didn't. I was just teasing." With any other woman, he would have reached for her hand. Not with Amanda. It was all he wanted, for now, that she trusted him enough to be alone with him.

"Where do you live?" she asked.

"Malibu. Straight up the coast."

"Okay," she said, settling back in the sports car's seat. "Lead on."

5

HE'D NEVER FELT MORE self-conscious in his life, taking her to his temporary home above the nightclub. Nick's at Night looked entirely different during the day, with the parking lot almost empty and the bright afternoon sun beating down on the weathered wood. The neon sign was off, the martini glass motionless and dull. And the only real sound was the crashing and hissing of the waves, and the traffic on Pacific Coast Highway.

Later, Sam would admit to himself that he shouldn't have worried at all. Because Hercule had been Mr. Hospitality himself, a charming host in short black fur. Never again would Sam underestimate a dog's ability to put the shyest of persons at ease.

He found himself babbling as he unlocked the door to his one-room dwelling. And one thing that Sam had never done in his life, up to this point in time, was babble.

"It's not always going to be this way," he said, turning the key in the lock and ushering her in ahead of him. "Just until I find Evan and get back on my feet..."

He watched her as she entered the large room, found himself wishing he could get inside her head for just an instant and know exactly what it was she was thinking as she gazed around the space that encompassed everything he owned in the world.

The leather couch looked like a pathetic excuse for a

bed. Like some college kid's dorm room. Sam cleared his throat. His mind had jumped to some erotic thoughts he'd had concerning himself, Amanda and that couch. He felt like the dirty dog he was, mentally undressing her that first night they met.

But lust was lust, and sometimes even preceded love. The male brain seemed to need a pretty gigantic signal to catch its attention. And he was the first person to believe that passionate feelings shouldn't be ignored. He was attracted to her, and now they were finally alone. Though he didn't intend to pounce on her just yet, he'd thought about making those moves—and all the moves that would come after.

Now, if he could just think of a way to make her relax, and get to know her better—

Just then Amanda's eye was caught by sudden movement on the leather couch. The sleeping bag undulated in little waves of motion. A small, ugly black head appeared, eyes button bright.

"Oh!" was all Amanda said. And in that moment, Sam deduced two very important things. Number one, that Amanda had always wanted a pet and had probably never had one. And two, that his little black bulldog utterly enchanted her.

"Amanda, meet Hercule. Hercule, let's go for our walk—"

The word *walk* was barely out of his mouth before Hercule darted off the couch. But instead of heading toward Sam, he made a beeline for Amanda.

"Traitor," Sam muttered under his breath.

She obviously loved the little dog—kneeling down and petting his head, smiling at him, then laughing as he panted up at her and swiped at her hand with his pink tongue. Hercule's doggy body fairly quivered with excitement. As much as he loved his walks, he loved company even more.

"Leash," Sam said, but Hercule didn't even spare him a glance. He was much more interested in Amanda. And Sam, as he reached for the bulldog's leash, found himself in the embarrassing position of being jealous of his own dog.

THEY WALKED ALONG THE beach, just a short distance north of the nightclub. Hercule barked at the seagulls and ran around in circles while Amanda tried to keep her emotions under control.

She'd never really been out on a date before. A shocking admission, but one that was not all that unusual, considering the upbringing she'd had. First, the private all-girl schools. Then the work schedule she'd maintained whenever she'd been home. A few times she'd asked her mother if she could go on vacation with Cindy, but Libby had always softly vetoed those requests.

So she had quietly existed, and if the normal hormones and female desires had flowed through her bloodstream and taken root in her heart, she hadn't known how to do anything about them. The habit of pleasing her mother had been far too deeply ingrained by then.

Oh, there had been group outings. Always carefully supervised. Various events at their country club. But always with her mother hovering in the background. Once, the summer she'd been sixteen, she'd struck up a friendship with her tennis instructor, and had felt that peculiar little frisson of excitement whenever he looked at her. But he'd left, to work at another exclusive club up in Carmel.

But those feelings were nothing compared to what she already felt for Sam.

Now, alone with this man, her mother nowhere in sight, Amanda quietly walked along the beach and tried to hide her inner turmoil. They could have been any couple in Los Angeles, out for a stroll with their dog, except for the fact that, for her, this was a truly unprecedented event.

He didn't try to talk to her right away, and she liked that about him. He simply walked along the shoreline, after having taken Hercule to a few of the hibiscus bushes by the nightclub's large parking lot. The little dog trotted by his side now, all the while glancing in her direction.

She found both dog and man absolutely irresistible.

HE WONDERED WHAT WAS going through her head, and didn't have a clue. Though Sam didn't consider himself an expert on women, with four sisters and the experience they had given him, he thought he had some insight into the feminine mind.

Now, walking the beach with Amanda, he found himself realizing that this was part of what drew him to her. She had the most incredible air of mystery about her. That, and a vulnerability that tore at his heart.

He'd seen that vulnerability when she'd knelt down and patted Hercule. The little bulldog had scrabbled against her, trying to climb into her lap. She'd laughed, put her arms around the quivering canine body, and Sam had melted at the expression on her face. It was the first time he'd seen her with her guard down.

He'd wondered what she could look like if she let down that guard and had some fun. Now he finally knew. Those incredible blue eyes had seemed lit from within. What had made them so beautiful, Sam realized, was that they no longer had that look of startled reserve. Her gorgeous lips had curved into a smile, and her cheeks had flushed a pleased pink.

Jealous of a dog... Man, you've got it bad....

WITH HERCULE THOROUGHLY exhausted and walked out, they headed back toward the nightclub. Once upstairs and inside the single room, Sam decided to play host.

"I've got soda, juice or beer. Which would you prefer?"

She seemed hesitant, and Sam quietly hoped she wouldn't insist he take her home right away. Walking Hercule had been a necessity. Anything else after that would be extra.

She looked across the room at him, and Sam forced himself to give her his most reassuring smile. He wanted to spend some time with her, away from Cindy, her mother, any of his friends. Even Hercule, who was now sitting in his favorite chair, eyeing Amanda as if she were another of his rubber play toys. The dog was infatuated with her.

"What kind of juice?" she finally asked.

"Orange or pineapple. But I know they've got cranberry and grapefruit down in the bar, if you'd rather have that."

"Oh, no. Orange will be fine."

He could see she wasn't a woman who would ever feel comfortable rocking the boat, asking for anything that would put another person out. The thought made him sad, somehow.

"Sure? It's just a quick run down to the bar."

She hesitated.

"It's no trouble."

He could read the indecision on her face. A face, he thought, that he would never grow tired of looking at.

"Cranberry, right?"

She glanced up at him, startled.

"How did you know?"

"You seem like a cranberry sort of person."

That brought the slightest of smiles to her face.

"I'll be right back." Sam let himself out the door and started along the walkway toward the wooden stairs.

HE MET NICK IN THE kitchen, trying out a new dish.

"Sam," his friend said, as he sautéed onions and garlic in the large, cast-iron frying pan. "I'm glad you're home. I was about to come up and see you, because I've got a few ideas about where Evan could have—"

"Not right now," Sam said, ducking his head inside one of the huge stainless-steel refrigerators and pulling out a bottle of cranberry juice.

"Hard at work on a case?"

"You might say that," Sam replied. He couldn't help smiling at the sight of Nick standing by the stove. Nick looked like the classic surfer and lifeguard. Tanned, his blond hair bleached even blonder by the sun, his biceps bulging beneath the bright blue T-shirt he wore over his faded jeans. Of course, he was barefoot.

"Try this sauce," Nick said, lifting the lid off another pot. Delicious aromas of tomato, basil and oregano filled the air.

"Can't. Not now." Sam glanced around the kitchen. "Have you got anything suitable for a snack? Not too heavy, we just had lunch. Maybe something like a dessert—"

"We?" Nick took the frying pan off the burner, stirring the onions as the heat died down, to prevent them from sticking to the bottom of the pan. "We, as in female? Sam, do you have a girl in your room?"

Sam felt all of twelve, even though he knew his friend didn't mean it that way. "Yes. And I want to get back to her as soon as possible."

"Go. Dessert, huh?" Nick thought about this, but Sam could tell from the mischievous light in his green eyes that his friend was amused that he finally had some feminine company. "Something chocolate for this lady, I think. Is it serious?"

"I want it to be."

"You've got it bad."

"Yeah. Dessert. Leave it outside the door after you knock."

"Don't I get to see her?"

"All right. Two minutes, tops. I'm not sure how long she's going to stay."

"Ah. So you like her, but she—"

Sam groaned. Nick was endlessly fascinated by people, a trait he'd inherited from his warmhearted father. Right now, Sam wished he had no interest in his love life.

"I'll help you out, buddy. I made the most incredible *tiramisù* this morning."

"Great. I'll come back down and—"

"Naw. I'll be right up."

AMANDA COULD HAVE sworn Sam was nervous as he left to get her cranberry juice. But that didn't make any sense. As a private detective, Sam must have been in many tight scrapes, so why would a simple afternoon at home be such a challenge?

She glanced down as she heard a doggy whine, and saw Hercule at her feet, the remote control in his mouth.

"TV?" she asked.

His little body quivered.

She took the remote out of his mouth and aimed it at the large-screen television that dominated one wall of the room. As she did, Hercule jumped into her lap, gave her face a quick swipe with his tongue, then settled in against her side.

A football game. Amanda glanced down at Hercule. He covered his face with his paws and sighed.

"No?" She switched the channel.

The news. "Too depressing," she told Hercule.

Another channel. A talk show, with an amazingly dysfunctional family. "Nope." She switched again.

Libby's World. On this particular episode, Libby was making the most elaborate centerpiece for a spectacular holiday dinner. Out of curiosity, Amanda glanced at Hercule. Again, the paws over the head, the beseeching expression in his bright black eyes.

"Not a winner. I agree." She pushed down the sharp stab of guilt at the thought of what her mother would think if she knew where she was—and with whom. Fought the guilt down with the thought that she was only visiting Sam, getting to know him. They could be friends, couldn't they? The roller-coaster climbs and dives her stomach had been taking gave the lie to that notion.

Amanda switched channels again, not wanting to think too much. Katharine Hepburn filled the screen, vibrant and vulnerable and so achingly beautiful. *Bringing Up Baby.*

Amanda didn't even have to look down. Hercule barked once, then twice, and snuggled against her as he hooked his two front paws over the front of the large chair-cushion. Amanda had to laugh.

"I agree." She set down the remote and sat back in the easy chair, all thoughts of her mother out of her mind.

As SAM LET HIMSELF back inside, the bottle of chilled cranberry juice in hand, he immediately registered the fact that the television set was on. Hercule was trustingly snuggled up against Amanda, and both of them were absorbed in Kate Hepburn and Cary Grant's screwball adventures.

Good thing the little furball doesn't have opposable thumbs, or he might have opened up a bottle of wine and turned on the stereo....

Sam walked over to the refrigerator, got out the ice tray.

Pretty pathetic when you're jealous of your own dog....

He poured two glasses of juice, set them on a tray, grabbed a dog biscuit for Hercule, and headed for the television area.

She glanced at him as he set the tray down, then gave Hercule his biscuit. The dog didn't even touch it.

"Hercule?"

The bulldog gazed up at his new friend, adoration in his eyes.

"Can I give it to him?"

Sam gritted his teeth. "Of course."

Normally, Hercule would grab the biscuit out of his hand in a most unseemly manner. Sort of like wrestling with shoes, another of his canine obsessions. Now, since the biscuit was proffered by a goddess, Hercule daintily took it out of Amanda's hand and even managed to crunch it up without making too much of a mess in the chair.

"He's so adorable!"

Sam sighed, then collected himself.

"Do you have any pets?"

"No." She hesitated. "I won a kitten once. At a church bazaar. But Mother— I had to give it back because..."

Sam didn't even hear the rest. His instincts had been right. At that moment, all jealousy toward Hercule faded away, because Amanda had been denied one of the most special experiences a child could ever have. He wondered how many other things Libby had denied her daughter.

The knock at the door startled them both.

"My friend. Nick," Sam tried to explain as he headed toward the door. "I thought we might have a little dessert while we watched the movie."

He opened the door and Nick stepped in, carrying a tray with two servings of *tiramisù* on pretty dishes, sprinkled with shaved chocolate and whipped cream. He'd also included a small pot of coffee, which smelled wonderful.

"I'll take that," Sam muttered.

"Nonsense. Just tell me where to put it."

Sam refrained from stating the obvious. After all, there was a woman in the room.

"The table in front of the television would be fine."

Nick placed the tray down, and Sam saw him swiftly sizing up Amanda. The rush of male possessiveness and swift jealousy that filled him absolutely astounded him. Nick was probably his best friend in the entire world. But that didn't mean he liked watching him check out Amanda.

"Amanda," Sam said quietly, "this is my friend, Nick Mangione. Nick, this is Amanda Hailey."

"Nice to meet you." Nick extended his hand, and Amanda took it and shook it. And Sam watched the entire exchange, feeling like a cranky two-year-old. He was flipping out, no doubt about it. First, jealous of his dog. Now, of his best friend. That he could be so possessive about a woman who he wasn't sure even wanted to be with him was a real revelation.

Once Nick left, Sam poured the coffee and set out the rich dessert. No diet stuff for Nick; he only used the best, freshest, richest ingredients. He watched as Amanda took her first bite, then smiled at the look of absolute ecstasy that washed over her face.

"This is wonderful."

"I know. Nick makes a mean *tiramisù*."

They watched the rest of the movie in silence, except for Hercule's occasional excited barks and whines. Then, as the credits rolled, Sam wondered what he was going to say.

The phone rang and saved him.

"Go ahead and get that," Amanda said, petting Hercule, who looked up at Sam with an expression of bliss on his wrinkled face.

"I'll be just a moment." He headed toward his desk,

then picked up the receiver as he settled himself into the chair. "The Blackthorne Agency, Sam Cooper here."

Mrs. Boswell.

"My dear boy, I got your message the other night."

He could hear the fear in her voice.

"I don't want you to give up," Sam said. "I've put ads in all the local papers, and posters up wherever I could. It's only a matter of time before the person who has Fifi realizes she belongs to someone else."

"I hope you're right. It's just that— Well, the longer she's away, the more that I think...the worst." Mrs. Boswell's voice crumpled, and Sam could picture her in her library, clutching the phone with one hand, a lace handkerchief in the other.

"Mrs. Boswell? Mrs. Boswell?" This was the part of his job that Sam truly hated. There were rare times he had to deliver bad news to his clients, and he couldn't stand hurting people, even though it wasn't his fault. Sometimes it was just the way of the world. Bad things could definitely happen to good people.

"Yes?" She blew her nose. "Oh, Sam, I'm so sorry to keep bothering you—"

"You're not a bother at all—"

"But I just miss my little girl."

"I know. I know." He thought of Mrs. Boswell, elderly and alone. Filthy rich, and with a group of relatives who were waiting for her to kick off so they could be the beneficiaries of all her hard work. Fifi had been her best friend, the most constant and loyal company the woman had. The poodle was also the only family member the old lady trusted.

"Mrs. Boswell," Sam said, "I want you to hold on while I check my E-mail. I put word out on the Internet

about Fifi, and I'm going to check and see if anyone's responded."

"Would you do that? Oh, my dear boy..."

He glanced over toward the door out of the corner of
his eye. Amanda had approached his desk, and now
stood within reach, clearly concerned.

"Can I help?" she asked.

He thought quickly. Mrs. Boswell seemed to be going
over the edge. "Talk to her while I check my messages.
She's just going through a bad time. Her poodle ran
away almost two weeks ago."

Amanda nodded her head and picked up the phone.

"Hello. Yes. No. This is Amanda. I'm a friend of
Sam's."

Sam typed away furiously on the keyboard as he half
listened to Amanda talking to his client. She had a wonderful telephone voice, low and soothing. He'd never
heard it before, and Sam realized she wasn't scared or
nervous talking to Mrs. Boswell. Her mind was occupied with the other person, so her self-consciousness
was completely forgotten.

Sam scanned his messages. Nothing. This would not
be good news for Mrs. Boswell. He left another general
message on the Net—an update on the poodle hunt—
then shut off the computer and turned to Amanda.

Any thoughts he had of getting the phone back from
her were quickly forgotten. She'd taken the portable
phone from his working area and was now sitting on
the couch, Hercule on her lap.

"Yes. Yes, I understand. Well, of course, you miss
her! It must be terrible not knowing where she is. Of
course. Of course."

Sam smiled. Some things just needed a woman's touch.

"Oh, I know that area. Really? I think I know the house. Is it the big pink one that looks like a castle?"

Sam blinked. How had Amanda gotten that close to Mrs. Boswell that fast?

"Of course! I used to drive past it all the time. I mean, my mother did, on the way to my ballet classes."

He watched her, curled up on the couch. She was totally absorbed in Mrs. Boswell and her problems. And a terrific listener. In other circumstances, Sam might have thought of hiring her on at the agency. Amanda, with her classic blond looks, could have infiltrated many situations in which his scruffy, alley-cat persona would just not have worked.

"I know. Loneliness is a terrible thing. Yes. Yes, I hate to eat alone, too." Amanda hesitated. "Oh, I know what you mean."

Sam scratched his head. He just didn't get it. Ten minutes on the phone with the woman, and Amanda had her life story, all her vulnerabilities, her deepest thoughts and fears. How did she do it?

"Tonight? I... Well, I—I'm not really sure...."

Sam watched her carefully. He had a feeling that Mrs. Boswell had just asked them both to her house for dinner. He'd shared a few glasses of Bordeaux with her in front of the fireplace, but never dinner. *Well.*

"I'll have to ask Sam," Amanda was saying.

Oh, he liked the sound of that. It implied they were a couple.

She cupped the mouthpiece with her hand. "Sam," she whispered. "She sounds really awful. Like the slightest little thing might send her over the edge. I think she's just in a really bad place right now."

Beautiful and exquisitely sensitive to boot, Sam thought.

"She wants us to come to dinner," Amanda continued. "I'm a little worried about her. She sounds desperate."

"If I know Mrs. Boswell, that could be the case," he replied. Though Sam knew the woman well enough to feel sure she wouldn't do anything truly desperate.

"What are we going to do?"

This was better than he could have expected. The afternoon *and* evening with Amanda. He would have to thank Mrs. Boswell for this later. After Fifi was returned.

"Well," said Sam. "It looks like we're going to dinner."

DINNER. ALONE WITH Amanda.

And Mrs. Boswell.

But, thought Sam as he swiftly changed into a more suitable shirt and casual jacket, any time he could spend with Amanda, getting her used to him, making her see him as someone she could spend the rest of her life with—well, that was all part of his master plan.

And after dinner, maybe he could persuade her to let him take her on a romantic drive up along Mulholland Drive, overlooking the City of Angels.

Anything was possible.

He came out of the bathroom, ready to go, and saw Amanda snapping Hercule's leash to his collar. The little dog was fairly quivering with excitement.

"Good idea. A short walk before we leave."

"Oh, no." She looked up at him, slightly flustered. "I thought we'd take him with us."

"What?"

She scooped Hercule up into her arms. "What Mrs. Boswell needs now, more than ever, is to have a dog in her arms. She needs Fifi, but Fifi isn't here right now, so Hercule will have to do."

Unfortunately, he had to admit her logic made sense.

"Have you discussed this with Mrs. Boswell?" he asked, knowing in his gut that he already had his answer.

"Of course. She's even directed her chef, Antoine, to grill him a chopped sirloin steak. She didn't think pasta would agree with him."

So there! Hercule seemed to be saying to him, doggy defiance emanating from his sleek black body. His dark eyes watched Sam keenly.

Sam sighed. There was no way Hercule could be left at home now. His vocabulary was small, but select. Along with the words *walk* and *leash,* he also unfortunately knew the words *sirloin* and *beef.*

One thing Sam had learned over the years of being a private detective was that there was a time and place to fold your hand of cards and simply give in.

This was one of those times.

"All right," he said. "Let's go."

"It looks a lot like Pickfair," Amanda said as the Miata made its way up Mrs. Boswell's flower-lined driveway.

Sam knew Amanda was referring to another mansion in Beverly Hills, once owned by the actress Mary Pickford and her husband, Douglas Fairbanks. And indeed,

Mrs. Boswell's mansion looked a lot like that famous Los Angeles landmark.

"Are you interested in architecture?" This was one of the main things he enjoyed about the time he spent with Amanda—getting to know every single thing about her.

"Yes. It fascinates me."

"Hmm." He opened the driver's-side door, and Hercule scrabbled over him, rushing to get out and smell those flowers—or do God knew what else to them.

"Hercule!" Sam grabbed the bulldog's leash. "Now, we've been invited to dinner and have to behave accordingly."

"Hercule," Amanda said as she came around the side of the sports car and took the leash gently out of Sam's hand. "Hercule, you're here on a mission of mercy. I want you to do your best to cheer Mrs. Boswell up."

Hercule, who had been sniffing a border of impatiens, turned toward Amanda and cocked his head at the sound of her voice.

"That's a good boy. I just want you to be your most charming self."

He barked happily and Sam closed his eyes.

Oh, brother.

He had a feeling that, even with Amanda at his side, it was going to be a long night.

AMANDA'S INSTINCTS had been dead-on. The sight of Hercule was like a balm to Mrs. Boswell's heavy heart. The woman brightened immediately, and by the time dessert was served, she was talking enthusiastically about what she was planning to do once they found Fifi.

Hercule eyed the chocolate mousse and gave Mrs.

Boswell his most charming doggy grin, but she was a canny old lady and wasn't buying it.

"Chocolate is so bad for dogs. Did you know that, Sam? Many a family pet has died when it sniffs out and devours a wrapped box of candy beneath the Christmas tree. My vet says their systems just can't handle it." She turned toward Amanda, diamonds glittering on her ears and fingers. "Darling, would you take that little scamp into the kitchen and ask Antoine to give him several of Fifi's best biscuits?"

"Of course." Amanda lifted a wiggling-in-protest Hercule into her arms and headed toward the immense kitchen at the back of the mansion.

"Sam," Mrs. Boswell said, as soon as Amanda was out of earshot. "I knew I recognized her from somewhere. It just took this old brain a few minutes to remember where. She's Libby Hailey's daughter, isn't she?"

Sam nodded.

"And engaged to that Marvin Burgess."

That got Sam's attention. He hadn't even considered Mrs. Boswell as a source in his file on Amanda. Now, seeing it laid out in front of him, so very obvious, he could have kicked himself.

"Yes."

"My God." Mrs. Boswell stared in the direction Amanda had taken toward the kitchen. "You must not let that happen."

Sam hitched his chair a little closer to hers. "Tell me about him, Mrs. Boswell."

She shook her head, a disgusted expression on her finely lined face. "Call me Lucille. What can Libby

Hailey be thinking, giving a charming girl like that away to a man like Marvin?"

"Why do you think she's arranging this marriage?" Sam asked, knowing Lucille Boswell would have a handle on the truth. The woman didn't strike him as a gossip, but as an individual who had a keen understanding of human nature.

"Money, my boy. Money. What was that movie, when that man kept saying, 'Follow the money'?"

"*All the President's Men*. Redford and Hoffman."

"That's the one." She leaned closer and whispered, as they both heard Hercule's excited barks and Amanda's approaching presence. "You follow the money, Sam, and you'll find out what Libby Hailey is really up to."

She swiftly composed her features as Amanda returned to the dinner table.

"NOW, I WANT THE TWO of you to come back very soon, and we can have another dinner party. We can sit out on the terrace if the weather isn't quite as brisk. Perhaps a brunch on Sunday." Mrs. Boswell was happily chattering away as she walked them to the car.

"I'd like that," Amanda said.

"So would I," Sam added.

Hercule merely licked the older woman's face. She had presented him with a sweater of Fifi's, claiming it was "much too cold for such a delicate little doggy to be out in such nasty weather without his overcoat." Privately, Sam thought his dog looked ridiculous in the forest-green sweater with bright-red yarn cherries all over it. But he hadn't wanted to hurt his client's feelings.

He opened the car door for Amanda, and settled both

her and Hercule into the passenger seat. Shutting the door, he turned toward Mrs. Boswell as she walked him around to the driver's side.

"Call me," she said, her voice very low so it wouldn't carry to Amanda on the night air. "I'll fill you in on our man Marvin."

"I will," he promised.

THE HARDEST PART OF the evening was saying goodbye to Amanda. With other women, there had come that time when he'd wanted to say goodbye, when he'd felt as though he wanted a break from their company. Even needed a breather.

Not with Amanda.

He hated having to drive her back to her mother's mansion. She asked him to drop her off almost a block away, but he'd insisted on seeing her to the door, even if that meant parking his car and walking with Hercule until they reached the imposing black gates.

"Thank you, Sam," she said quietly as they reached the estate entrance. "I had a wonderful day."

He sensed that her mother had been off on some project, and hadn't even noticed that her daughter hadn't been home for dinner.

"I did, too." There were so many other things he wanted to say, but he didn't know where to begin. He cleared his throat, thought about taking her hand, then looked down at her, knowing what he was feeling had to be in his eyes, in his expression, when she said—

"But I can't ever see you again."

Hercule whined and leaned up against Sam's leg.

"What?"

"I can't see you again."

"Amanda, wait a minute—"

"*Please*, Sam, don't ask me to."

Who was it who said desperate times called for desperate measures? Before she could walk away from him, Sam grabbed her arm, turned her into his embrace, lowered his head and kissed her, all the while hoping she wouldn't struggle, break away and slap him silly.

She didn't. She stiffened at first, in surprise, then she melted against him, unleashing emotion so strong he almost shook with it. Dimly, in the back of his mind, the part not totally consumed with this kiss, he realized she'd been bottled up for so long that no wonder it all came roaring out of her like this.

Her hands slid up into his hair, his slid more tightly around her waist. And Hercule, still on his leash, walked around and around them, tangling their legs together with his leather leash.

Good dog, Sam thought as he tasted her lips again. Maybe Rick had let Ilse go, but he sure wasn't going to make the same mistake with Amanda. There were some things in life far too precious to be sacrificed, and love was one of them.

She broke away, disentangling herself from Hercule's leash, breathing as if she'd been exerting herself. He felt his own heart pounding like he'd just run a four-minute mile in two. She stared up at him as if he'd grown another head, shock on her face, shock that he guessed came from the way her body had responded to his. And Sam knew that the body didn't lie.

His, at the moment, was uncomfortably and blatantly telling the truth. And he was quite sure she'd felt it.

He let her go only because he sensed she needed some time. He would find a way to see her again, and soon. So Sam watched as Amanda turned and swiftly let herself in the side gate. He watched through the black iron bars as she half ran up the drive, her blond hair the only light in the evening dusk. Then she disappeared around a corner.

He'd never felt so alone in his life. Like half of him had disappeared. As if in answer to his mood, a misty rain began to fall as he and Hercule walked back to the Miata. Sam settled his dog in the passenger seat, then put up the top of the sports car before getting in himself. Once inside, he turned on the heater and sat, thinking, as he scratched Hercule's head.

Hercule whined and licked his hand.

What now?

He gazed out the windshield, misty with rain. The street in front of him, the streetlights and the trees, all blurred.

Think.

He thought.

Aha! Mrs. Boswell.

He pictured Amanda as she'd looked at dinner tonight.

"I'll fill you in on our man Marvin...."

"No time like the present," he said to Hercule as he started the car.

6

SAM ALWAYS THOUGHT best as he drove. Now, heading west on the Santa Monica Freeway toward Malibu, he reviewed everything Mrs. Boswell had told him about Marvin Burgess and Libby Hailey.

Not a nice pair of people. Totally self-centered and uncaring of whose life they ruined in the process. The world revolved around these two narcissists.

And Amanda was caught in the middle.

"I can't ever see you again...."

At first, pain and fear had twisted his gut. He couldn't begin to believe he would never see her again. So he'd consciously slowed down, gotten a grip, and gone into his analyzing mode.

He'd heard the fear in those words. Sensed it. And if he'd thought for one minute that this was what Amanda really wanted, he would have left her alone. For good. But he didn't buy it. Instead, he saw a frightened young girl trapped in the body of a young woman. An individual who had scarcely been allowed to spread her wings and fly before they'd been rudely clipped. His Amanda was not going to be held prisoner in that gilded cage any longer than was necessary.

Besides, what Mrs. Boswell had told him about Marvin Burgess was *very* interesting....

AMANDA STOOD ON HER bedroom balcony and stared out into the cool evening. The slight rain had washed everything clean, and now she gazed into the darkness, unseeing, as she remembered every single detail of how Sam had kissed her.

There had been no warning. She'd tried to walk away, rejecting what he'd been trying to do since the moment they met, when finally he'd pulled her into his arms.

A part of her had wanted him to. A part of her wanted to do more than kiss Sam, wanted him in a way she'd never wanted Marvin. Or any man.

And another part of her was scared to death.

SAM CALLED CINDY as soon as he got home and filled her in on his day with Amanda. But he held back what he'd learned from Mrs. Boswell. He'd promised her total anonymity. And he said nothing about the kiss.

"Amanda's scared," Cindy said. "Scared of what she feels for you. But that's good. Now, what we've got to do is rely on her perception of fate."

"Fate?" Sam questioned. Always a man who respected women's intuition, he waited for Cindy to fill him in.

"Okay. It was fate that you saw her at the Beverly Wilshire Hotel, and fate that you overheard our cellphone conversation. And sheer determination on your part that you crashed our lunch. Then I had a hand in letting you know about the movie and the computer shopping."

"So you're going to help fate along again?"

"Yep. Amanda believes in the concept of fate. Hey, I do, too. We read romance novels by the boxful while we were at boarding school, and fate's always a major player in those stories."

"Hmm," Sam mused. "Just like in the old movies."

"Exactamento. Now, call me crazy, but I snuck a look at her Day Runner while she went to the bathroom at the computer store. I offered to hold her bag for her."

Sam laughed. "You're sure you don't want a job with The Blackthorne Agency?"

"Nope. I've got too much capital tied up in fabric painting. Anyway, Amanda has an art class a few days from now, one that she loves and never misses."

Sam grabbed a pen and jotted down the particulars.

In the meantime, he had work to do.

AFTER HIS LAST conversation with Mrs. Boswell, Sam had a lot more to go on. He spent the next two days gathering information and making up a master list. He'd done enough calling around so that he had a complete file on every single business Libby was employing to pull off this masterpiece of a wedding.

He knew that today was the day Amanda's wedding dress was to be delivered. He also knew who the driver was. And he knew he was going to bribe the guy and get inside that house. Get another look at Libby Hailey. Find a few more pieces of the puzzle, as all good detectives did.

The van left Some Enchanted Evening, a store devoted to gorgeous wedding dresses, at exactly ten o'clock in the morning, with Sam in hot pursuit. He followed the van cautiously until it turned onto one of the side streets on the way to the Hailey estate.

Sam went into action.

Honking his horn and waving his hand, he made

enough of a commotion that the driver, a portly Mexican of indeterminate age, pulled over.

He walked back to the Miata as Sam jumped out of the car.

"Are you in trouble?"

"No, no. But you see, the dress you're delivering is for my fiancée, Amanda Hailey."

The driver walked back to his van, checked the invoice, then nodded his head. "Yes."

"I'd like to deliver it in person."

The driver smiled, then shook his head. "I cannot do that. If you run off with the dress, it will be my job. On the line, you know?"

"I know. That's why I'd like to follow you to the Hailey estate, and you can drop me off and watch me go to the front door with the dress. I swear, I just want to surprise my fiancée."

"But you are not supposed to see the bride before the wedding."

"I can see the dress. But not her dressed in the dress." Sam hoped that last line had made sense.

The driver considered this. Scratched his head. Then he smiled, and Sam knew he had him. Thank God there were a few romantic souls left in the world.

"Okay. But I follow you there, and I watch you go to the door and ring the bell. I don't leave until the dress is checked in and everything is complete. Then I'll let you go in and deliver it."

"Fine by me."

SAM KNEW, FROM consulting with Cindy, that Amanda wasn't home; Cindy had come by earlier to take her shopping. And he doubted that Libby would recognize him from their little meeting at the Beverly Wilshire Hotel. A judicious use of spirit gum, a false mustache and some extra false teeth made him look nothing at all like the man who had swept her daughter onto the dance floor.

Being something of a master of disguise was all in a day's work for any member of The Blackthorne Agency.

Now he had to infiltrate the premises.

Miguel was as good as his word. He drove the company van right up to the gates, after letting Sam park his Miata a mere half-block away and swing up into the passenger side of the pale blue van.

"This is crazy," the man muttered as the gates opened and they drove up to the house and parked. "But I was in love once, too."

"Oh, don't say anything to her mother, because she doesn't like me."

"No kidding? Same with my mother-in-law."

"Then you understand."

"But won't she recognize you?"

Sam pulled gently at the false mustache, then yanked at the bill of his baseball cap, causing it to slide down lower and conceal more of his face.

"Ah! So you are a true romantic, I see!"

"The last of a dying breed."

A uniformed maid answered the door, then went to get Libby Hailey. Sam stood patiently by while Libby signed for the dress, then Miguel left him with a wink.

"Where would you like me to put this?" Sam asked.

"Oh, it's not necessary," Libby replied, with a queen-of-the-manor air. "I'll just have Maria take it up to my daughter's room."

"Oh, nonsense," Sam said, putting on his best interior-decorator-and-caterer air. "I'll just take it up in a jiff, make sure it's all settled in her closet, and let myself out. My partner's waiting in the van, and it'll only take a sec."

Libby eyed him, clearly seeing total riffraff.

Sam gave her a big, toothy grin.

"All right. But make it quick. I'll send Maria to show you the way." She turned and started down the long entranceway.

Sam waited until she was out of sight, then signaled to Miguel that he could leave with a quick thumbs-up. Miguel started the van and drove down the drive toward the main gate as Sam turned toward the maid.

Maria was a round woman, all smiles and gentle eyes.

"This way, please."

He followed her up the stairs, down an impressive hallway flanked with small oil paintings and several vases on pedestal stands. But Sam didn't have much time for more than a quick look before she was showing him inside a bedroom.

"The closet is there," she said, pointing.

"The dress is exquisite," Sam said. "Don't you think Miss Hailey will be a beautiful bride?"

Maria hesitated, and Sam realized the woman saw the truth all too clearly.

"I hope she will be happy" was all the maid said before she turned and quietly left the bedroom.

Sam hung the dress in the closet, fluffing out the voluminous, fairy-princess-like skirt so the material wouldn't wrinkle. He glanced around the bedroom.

Beautifully decorated. Neat as a pin. It had Libby's

personality all over it, and, as far as he could see, none of Amanda's.

Working swiftly, he reached into the knapsack he'd carried inside and took out the single red rose he'd carefully wrapped in tissue. Laying it on the pillowcase, along with the little note he'd written, he concealed the single flower with another pillow, propped at an angle. Then he left the bedroom, closing the door softly behind him.

HE'D PROWLED THROUGH a lot of houses before, and had never been caught. He already had an excuse locked and loaded, that "the house was so immense I just got lost, and looking at the wonderful things you did with the window treatments, well..."

Sam hesitated before he crossed in front of what had to be a large library as he heard Libby talking. Did she have company he didn't know about? The sky outside was overcast, cloudy and gray, and Libby had a fire crackling in the opulent marble fireplace.

Sam leaned closer, the better to hear what was being said over the snapping and hissing of the flames.

"So then the transaction has been completed," he heard Libby say.

Big pause. Pause. Pause.

She was talking on the telephone.

Sam took a quick peek inside. Libby was sitting in front of the fire, with a cup of tea and a slice of cake. The lady of the manor.

"Thank you very much."

Sensing this particular conversation was about to end, Sam snuck down the hall and out the front door.

Mission accomplished, even though he still didn't know what Libby had been talking about.

AMANDA LET HERSELF into her bedroom, then set her armload of shopping bags down at the foot of the bed. Walking into her bathroom, she pulled her hair back, splashed cool water on her face, dried off, then returned to her bedroom where she slipped out of her peach sundress and slid on her robe.

Early evening, just before dinner—and she was exhausted.

Oh, she'd had fun with Cindy. Her friend had attempted to keep the morning and afternoon lighthearted and fun. Lots of laughs. Amanda had gone along with it, all the while feeling a terrible turmoil inside.

Now, as she studied the shopping bags at the foot of her bed, she knew she would have returned each item, even most of the clothing in her closet, for a chance at...

At what?

Instantly, Sam's face came to mind. The kiss.

She closed her eyes. Pushed the memory down. One thing she'd learned long ago was that it did no good to pine after something you just couldn't have. To long for something that was as out of your reach as the moon in the night sky.

"Amanda?"

She recognized her mother's voice and schooled her features into a semblance of relative calm before turning to face the woman who had given birth to her.

"Mother."

"Did you have a nice day?"

"Very nice."

"Where did you and Cindy go?"

"All over. Mostly Beverly Hills."

"I can see that by your shopping bags." Libby was never so happy as when she was purchasing things, and now Amanda watched as her mother knelt down and foraged into the various bags.

"Just think, darling, when you're married to Marvin you'll be able to buy anything you want."

Amanda studied her mother, and was astonished at the rush of emotion that welled up inside her, lodging at the back of her throat as she fought against speaking the words.

Mother, I think I may really be in love. I didn't know what that felt like before I agreed to marry Marvin, but now I don't think I can go through with this marriage. I want to see Sam again. He kissed me, and...I want to know where it can all lead to. It may lead to nothing, but I have to know—

"This is very cute," Libby said, holding up a pale pink, cotton sweater set. "And that dress is smart enough to go with you on your honeymoon. I think Marvin said something about the Caribbean island of Mustique. That palazzo that used to belong to Princess Margaret. He said he might rent it for a few weeks. And that I might even come down for a long weekend."

The thought of spending a few weeks in the Caribbean with Marvin, his friends, and even her mother brought Amanda absolutely no joy. She looked at Libby as she brought out yet another dress and laid it on the bed, complimenting her on her color choice, and wondered what it would be like to have a mother she could sit out in the garden with, really talk to, while they shared a cup of tea.

She knew, from long and painful experience, that it

wasn't going to happen. So Amanda sat on the edge of her bed in her ivory silk robe and watched as her mother oohed and aahed over her purchases.

There was nothing Libby liked more than *things*. She bought things. She encouraged her followers to buy things. To make things.

Amanda had nothing against surrounding herself with beautiful things. She just didn't believe that possessions came before people. Before happiness and laughter and—

Love. Before love.

"Darling, you look pale. Shall I tell Maria to bring you up a little something? A cup of tea?"

"That would be wonderful." She'd reached maximum overload with her mother and needed some time away from her. Amanda felt herself relax as Libby walked briskly out of the bedroom.

She was about to lie back on the pillows when she noticed that one was at an odd angle. She lifted it, trying to position it in a more comfortable manner, and caught sight of the single red rose lying on top of another pillow. And a small white envelope with her name on it.

Her heartbeat sped up as she reached for the note. Opened it. Read the single line in a second.

Never, ever, is an awfully long time. Sam

She didn't have the luxury of reading it a second time. Or wondering how it had been delivered. Amanda knew her mother couldn't be allowed to see this, so she tucked the note into one of the side pockets of her Day Runner, then took the single red rose and placed it in a glass of water in her bathroom shower stall. She pushed down the intense rush of happiness and was more than composed when her mother returned, Maria at her heels.

"She has some soup for you, darling. Tomato bisque, your favorite. And a sandwich, with homemade bread. Did you even bother to stop for lunch?"

"I...no. I grabbed a muffin—"

"Well, no wonder you look pale." Libby directed Maria to set the tray down on the table by the bed. "Now, I want you to eat all of this, and then later on Maria will bring up your dinner." Libby smiled down at her daughter. "Did I tell you your wedding dress was delivered today?"

Amanda didn't know what to say. Any other bride would have rushed to the closet, wanted to look at her dress and spin romantic dreams for her future.

She didn't even want to admit it was there.

With a surge of emotion, she realized she couldn't pretend to be happy with this wedding anymore.

"Don't you want to see it?"

Maria stood by the door, her eyes downcast.

"Not really," Amanda said quietly.

She might never have voiced her opinion, for Libby went to the closet and brought the wedding dress out in all its glory. Amanda began to eat her soup.

"I think this neckline is just so cunning, don't you agree, darling?"

Amanda said nothing, wishing all the while that her mother would leave so she could get Sam's note out and study it. That note held more promise for her future than any wedding dress possibly could. But she didn't want to tip her mother off to the fact that anything was the matter, so Amanda forced herself to look at a dress she'd suddenly decided never to wear, and to feign the proper enthusiasm.

"It's lovely," she said.

SAM FOUND OUT EXACTLY what Libby's "transaction" had been all about within hours after his visit to the Hailey estate.

"Sam," his friend Ellroy Hornsby said when he called late that night, "you'd better come over here right away."

"Can't you tell me over the phone?"

"I'd rather not."

Ellroy was a computer genius. He could hack anything, break any code, find information with such breathless speed that he left others in the dust. Sam had helped him out of a jam once, and had persuaded this man who so easily could have turned to a life of crime and excitement that he was just what The Blackthorne Agency needed.

In his early thirties, Ellroy looked much older. Sam often thought he'd been born with his carefully combed thinning hair, wire-rimmed glasses, mild expression, and always-present pocket protector.

He'd asked Ellroy to do some checking on Libby Hailey. Especially concerning today's "transaction."

"Bank account," Ellroy said the minute Sam entered his cluttered studio apartment in the Valley. "My first instinct was correct. A cool million, Sam. From that Burgess guy."

"My God." Sam thought about this. The implications were staggering. "How did you—forget it, I don't want to know."

"I didn't move any numbers around. The money's all

still there. Just in and out, got the information, no one knows I was there. But Marvin Burgess deposited a cool million dollars into Libby Hailey's account this morning. That was what her transaction was all about."

Sam thought about this as Ellroy handed him a beer, then reached for one himself.

"Mind if I sit here for a minute and drink this?" he asked the computer consultant. He wasn't at all sure his legs would hold him if he stood suddenly.

"Not at all. I'm just going to get back to work."

Sam sipped his beer and thought, as Ellroy tapped on his keyboard, his attention on the softly glowing screen.

"I HAVE TO GET HER AWAY now," he told Hercule over dinner. "This is no longer just about me. This is about doing what's right."

Hercule, his head deep in his bowl, offered no comment.

The only thing Sam had decided, while deep in thought at Ellroy's apartment, was that Amanda could never know about the million dollars. It would hurt her too much, and Sam wanted the hurt to stop. He and Ellroy were the only two people on the planet, other than Libby and Marvin, who knew what had gone down. And the bank officers, of course.

It would stay that way.

"She doesn't need to know," Sam said, scratching Hercule's head.

AMANDA LOVED HER evening art classes. Her watercolors were about the only thing she did that her mother approved of. Amanda had started taking classes while in school, and had showed something of an aptitude.

She loved the whole atmosphere of the class, even down to the different textures of the papers and the brilliant washes of color.

It was one of the only places where she felt totally relaxed. At home. She knew her way around a brush and paper, and she loved translating what she saw in nature into a watercolor.

She'd taken lessons from Mrs. Wimberly since she was in her early teens, when she'd been home from boarding school for the summer. The woman seemed ageless—somewhere in her sixties for as long as Amanda had known her. Her teacher's passion for art kept her moving briskly throughout the class, tapping one student on the shoulder, whispering to another. Her only objective was to bring out the best in each of her students.

She taught out of her luxurious Japanese-style home in Brentwood, and her gardens and the pond filled with koi in back were as spectacular as the dramatic paintings that graced the interior of the house.

Now, setting up her work area, taking out various tubes of watercolor she would need for that evening, Amanda glanced up as Mrs. Wimberly entered the room, resplendent in a flowing caftan in jewel tones of turquoise, emerald and gold. Her silvery hair was pulled back sleekly into a tight knot, and dramatic Navajo jewelry graced her wrists and ears.

Amanda had been meaning to ask her teacher a question about a specific technique she wanted to try, but the question died in her throat when she saw who followed her. Not five steps behind, walking quickly to keep up with Mrs. Wimberly's brisk stride, was Sam Cooper.

HE DIDN'T DARE LOOK AT Amanda. If the truth were told, he was slightly intimidated by her teacher, this woman, this artist, this Mrs. Wimberly. She'd grilled him relentlessly as to why he wanted to attend her particular class, as Cindy had assured him she would. He'd tried to give her all the right answers, but now, in class, Sam was a bit intimidated. After all, the last artistic endeavor he could remember making was a finger painting in kindergarten. That was, if you didn't count houses and fences. Or being fingerprinted yourself.

Cindy had given him a few pointers as to what he should say. She'd taken several classes with the woman, and pronounced her absolutely the best. But now her attention was more on painting fabric than actual paintings.

"Let's set you up right here," Mrs. Wimberly was saying.

The gods were working in his favor. The spot she'd selected was right next to Amanda.

"Amanda, could I impose upon you to help our new student set up? Sam Cooper, Amanda Hailey. Now, we'll be starting on time, and as you always come a bit early—"

"Of course," Amanda replied. "It's no problem."

Well, Sam thought, at least she didn't look disgusted. Stunned would be more like it. Perhaps his and Cindy's plan had a chance of working, after all. Cindy had helped him find his way to this particular watercolor class, but fate itself had placed them side by side.

"Amanda," he said, and the note of wonder he injected into his voice was genuine. She looked beautiful, in a long, pale blue knit dress that reached the middle of her calves. On most women it would have looked dumpy. On her, it seemed ethereal.

"Sam," she said. She actually smiled at him. Her voice sounded remarkably steady. Happy, even. "Let's get you set up."

THE FIRST HALF OF THE class was devoted to individual work. The second half, according to Mrs. Wimberly, was left free for art appreciation. A painting would be set up at the front of the spacious studio, and each student would take a turn analyzing why it worked—or didn't.

The first half of the class had been painful for Sam. He'd sneaked several peeks at the others' efforts, especially Amanda's, and knew himself for the rank amateur he was. His drawings looked like the stick-figure artwork found in a preschool compared to what some of these students were turning out.

He wasn't too upset when Mrs. Wimberly announced the half-time break and asked everyone to clean up. After she had served tea from an absolutely stunning Japanese tea set, another student helped her position a painting at the front of the large, light-filled studio.

Several of the other students took turns giving the class their interpretations while Sam studied the work. He was of the school of "I don't know art, but I know what I like." Somehow, Sam knew that wouldn't be enough for this teacher.

"Sam?" Mrs. Wimberly prompted, bringing him into the discussion. He'd known this moment was coming, and had been thinking up his response. The only thing he knew to do was to speak directly from his emotions, as that was the way he always experienced any form of art.

"I'm not sure how the artist achieved this particular effect," he began, plunging right in. Sam had always believed that if you were going to make a complete and utter fool of yourself, you might as well jump in feet first. No testing the water for him.

"What I saw at first was a bunch of pastels, which might have given me the impression that this painting was delicate. Lacking in substance. It could have seemed rather light. But when I continued to look at it, when I went past my first, surface reaction, I realized there's a great deal of passion and power here. A great, untapped well of it, which seems to be waiting to be released."

He finished. Waited. Utter silence.

Open mouth, insert—

"Well." Mrs. Wimberly paused, studying him. Tapping her chin with her index finger. "Sam, I have to admit, you surprise me. I thought you were one of those men in Los Angeles who believed an art class might be an inventive way of—how is it said these days?—picking up chicks."

Someone behind them coughed, clearly covering a laugh.

"But you've obviously given this some thought."

Sam hesitated, then looked straight at Amanda.

"Well, you see, I've never believed that looks are all of it. Sometimes, with a painting, as with a person, you have to look beneath the surface at all the complexities to see what's really going on."

He didn't hold her gaze in an aggressive manner, but simply looked away, and then back at his teacher.

"Well," Mrs. Wimberly remarked. "That was very well said." She looked around the room, with the air of an ancient Egyptian queen addressing her subjects. Kind but firm, and with a bit of distance.

"Let's call it a night."

Sam finally let his breath out, then covertly eyed Amanda. The class might be over, but there was still the chance of a conversation outside by their cars, and perhaps a cup of coffee to be had.

After all, a faint heart never won a darn thing....

7

HE CAUGHT UP WITH HER at her car—the beige Mercedes, the same car he'd seen her in that first night, by the Beverly Wilshire Hotel.

"Amanda!"

She turned, and when she looked up at him, Sam realized she was no longer the cool and composed woman he'd seen before. She looked wary, but expectant. Her eyes seemed lit from within with a sort of energy he instantly recognized.

Something had changed.

He didn't stop to analyze it. He didn't question it. In Sam's line of work, he relied on his instincts. And he knew things could change within a heartbeat; an entire case could turn on one piece of information. People could change their minds. Lives could change direction in an instant.

He didn't question it because he didn't want to. So Sam lowered his watercolor case to the curb, moved closer, took her into his arms, and did what he'd wanted to do from the moment he'd first seen her, what he'd already done and was about to do again.

He kissed her.

THE FEELINGS SHE HAD for this man overwhelmed her.

His lips barely brushed hers, so it was a gentle kiss. But the energy around them, so electric, so fierce, so *alive*, enveloped her in a world that could encompass only Sam.

He didn't try to tease her lips apart, didn't force his tongue into her mouth. He simply touched his lips to hers, kissing her, wooing her, letting her lean against his hard, strongly muscled body. Letting her enjoy the feeling of those arms around her.

For that moment in time, she forgot everything about her life up to the present moment, and let Sam be her rock.

The kiss ended, the brief contact of his lips on hers broken. She felt as if she were struggling to come up for air. From what seemed like a very long distance, a car door slammed. Another car started up. And all Amanda could do was look up into Sam's face.

He seemed as shaken as she was.

She smiled.

"Oh, hell," he said softly. Then he kissed her again.

Afterwards, he took her out for coffee, to a romantic little Italian place on Robertson. The café had tables outside, and twinkling white lights surrounded the front of the restaurant. He had a double espresso, while she had a caffe latte, and as both of them talked, Amanda felt as if she were being swept away on the warmest and gentlest of tides. But she wasn't afraid, because she realized she was exactly where she wanted to be.

He told her about his family, his mother and father and five siblings. His oldest sister Thea, and her children. She could tell he adored his various nieces and nephews, and that he was close to his parents and siblings. His family sounded like a fiercely loyal clan, their holidays and get-togethers hilariously fun. By her second cup of Italian coffee and a serving of *tiramisù*, she realized it was the family she had always longed for but never had.

The night with Sam was misty and cool with the promise of more rain, dark and magical. Surrounded by those twinkling lights, oblivious to the other people and looking into Sam's eyes, Amanda knew it would be impossible for her to go through with the wedding her mother had arranged.

Her heart had decided otherwise. She knew she belonged with Sam.

THE NEXT DAY, EARLY in the evening, Amanda stared at the white wedding dress in her spacious bedroom closet and knew she couldn't marry Marvin.

Not after Sam's kisses.

Not after those kisses that had shown her, tantalized her with the promise of what she could feel for a man. No, not a man. *Sam*. What she could feel for Sam.

She stared at the dress, so incredibly beautiful, and hoped that someday another woman would wear it as she walked down the aisle. She felt a little sorry for the dress, but knew she would never use it.

It was time for her to leave home. Past time.

She'd known this moment was coming, in the back of her mind, from the instant Sam had danced with her. Before he'd even told her he was the man she was going to marry. She'd thought he was insane then, had tried to laugh it off. But as things had progressed, she'd realized that life, and fate, had a funny way of placing exactly what you needed right in front of you, if you were smart enough to see it.

She was smart, all right. But she'd also been scared a great deal of her life. Therefore, in her estimation, fate, or the universe, or the gods, or whatever you chose to call it, had thrown Sam in front of her a good many times.

Until he'd kissed her.

She touched her lips, remembering. Each little detail. The fast tempo of his heart beneath her fingertips. His slightly ragged breathing when he'd pulled away. The way her heart had pounded so loudly the last time, she'd been convinced every student still on the residential street could hear it.

His kisses had changed everything. She felt as if she'd been awakened from the deepest of metaphorical slumbers, and was now taking a good long hard look at her life.

She found it wanting. Any life without Sam would be wanting.

Amanda knew she had to leave. Now. Before she lost her nerve and changed her mind. After all, how many more times would Sam appear out of nowhere?

Getting up off her bed, Amanda headed toward her closet and the matched set of expensive luggage at the far end.

She packed two large suitcases, a trunk and an overnight bag. Very few clothes, mostly the possessions she considered near and dear. Photo albums. Scrapbooks. A few framed photos. Treasured books. The afghan her grandmother had made her, so many Christmases ago.

Then she called a taxi. She wouldn't take the Mercedes. The car had never felt like it belonged to her, and it was registered in her mother's name so she could use it to track her. No, this break had to be clean and final. For now. In a small corner of her heart, she hoped her mother might eventually forgive her, but Amanda was nothing if not a realist. Her life had shaped her, and she knew what her mother was capable of. It hurt her, to leave this way, but she knew instinctively that it would hurt her more to stay.

The cabdriver helped her bring her luggage down, loaded it in the trunk and the back seat. The wind had picked up, and as Amanda walked down the drive, it seemed as if even the weather was pushing her toward a new life. The tops of trees, of palms, bent, the wind rattling through the palm fronds, whispering through the leaves.

She gave the cabdriver Cindy's address, took one last look at the mansion that had been her summer and holiday home, and got inside the cab's front passenger seat, looking straight ahead.

She knew she couldn't look back.

FOR ONCE IN HER LIFE, Amanda rendered her friend speechless. Cindy said nothing. She simply stared as the cabbie unloaded the two large suitcases, overnight case and trunk. Amanda paid him, tipped him handsomely, then asked him not to tell anyone where he'd taken her.

"You in some kind of trouble?" the cabbie asked. He had steel-gray hair and kind blue eyes.

"No. But I need some time alone."

The cabbie gave her a long look, then replied, "You have a good Christmas, then."

Amanda smiled. "I think I will."

"This is the first place your mother will look," Cindy said as the cab left. "We've got to find you a better hiding place."

"Where?" Amanda hadn't thought that far ahead. It

had taken all her strength and willpower to leave in the first place. It had never crossed her mind that her mother might come looking for her at her friend's and cause a disturbance.

"Did you leave her a note?"

"No."

"Nothing?"

"I didn't know what to say. She'll know once she takes a look at my bedroom. It's not...in order."

"When is she due back?"

"Late. She had a charity dinner in Beverly Hills. There's an auction afterward, and she's in charge."

"Then we've got some time. Let me make a few phone calls."

"SAM," CINDY SAID from the privacy of her bedroom. She clutched the phone nervously. "Come to my house ASAP. Amanda's run away."

She heard a second of stunned silence, then a swift, "I'm on my way."

"I CALLED SAM," Cindy announced as she came into the kitchen.

Amanda, who hadn't been eating well at all the last few days, had found she suddenly had a ravenous appetite. Alice had made her a turkey sandwich with all the trimmings. She'd only taken about two bites, and the mention of Sam's name caused her stomach to flutter so badly she set it down.

"Sam?"

"You might have decided to ditch his card, but I didn't! Remember, he said to call if you ever needed him? Well, no time like the present."

"But I can't—"

"Yes, you can. The man's solid gold, and best of all, your mother has no idea where he lives. You can hide out with him until she finally gets it through her head that this time you're serious."

"But he won't—"

"He will. He is. He's on his way."

SAM BORROWED NICK'S Jeep, and reached Cindy's house in record time. With swift economy, he loaded Amanda's two suitcases, her trunk and her overnight bag into the back of the vehicle, then Cindy urged them to leave.

"Not that I don't love you guys, and the company," she said. "But just in case Libby comes home early, I don't want the two of you to be sitting ducks in the driveway."

"Good thinking," Sam said.

"Also," Cindy continued, "Alice and I are the only two people who know you've been here. I can trust Alice not to talk, but my brothers should be home pretty soon, and they might slip up."

Sam opened the passenger door for Amanda and she climbed in. As he approached the driver's side, Cindy tapped his arm.

"Be careful, Sam. Libby's not going to like this."

"I know."

You don't know the half of it, he thought as he drove around the circular driveway, then down and out into the residential street.

AMANDA DIDN'T SAY A WORD as they drove through Beverly Hills. Sam turned right on Sunset Boulevard and

headed toward the beach. He wasn't going to push her
into polite conversation, especially considering that kiss
after the art class that had knocked his socks off the
night before.

He'd had his share of experience. He didn't know
what had affected him more deeply—her sense of total
innocence, or the fact that she had gone into that second
kiss with complete trust. That first time, he'd insisted.
Pushed right past her caution. She'd wanted to leave
him, but he hadn't let her walk away that easily.

But that second time. In that simple, heartfelt moment in front of her art teacher's home, she'd given him
everything.

The thought of ever being able to make love to her,
the two of them alone and naked in bed, the images of
how she would give over to him that way just about
brought him to his knees emotionally.

But Sam knew he couldn't take advantage of this situation. He was the one who'd been around the proverbial block before, so he knew he had to protect her. Re-
assure her. Let her know she was in safe hands. Hands
that weren't going to try and slip beneath her skirts at
the first opportunity.

"Amanda," he said. They'd passed the San Diego
Freeway, and were now driving through Brentwood on
their way to Malibu. "I want you to know that I won't
take advantage of this situation. I know that what you
need is a safe place to hide. The kind of place where you
can lick your wounds and figure out what you're going
to do next."

The look she gave him was so grateful, his throat
tightened.

"I can only offer you a corner of my room right now,

but we'll rig up some walls with a couple of blankets and rope. You'll have your privacy, though Hercule might want to jump up and sleep with you."

"That would be okay," she said.

Her voice was so soft. He didn't have a clue as to what she might be thinking. He only knew that she'd done the most courageous thing in leaving her mother's house. It might not be on the same level as going off to war or being a street person and living precariously from day to day, but Sam knew exactly how sheltered Amanda had been. And therefore, how much it had cost her to leave the only home she'd ever known.

"Amanda," he said quietly, "I think that what you did today was incredibly brave, and I want you to know that I admire you for it."

She was silent for such a long moment, he wondered if she was going to answer. He glanced at her profile, and saw quick tears shimmering in those blue eyes before she looked away, gazing out the passenger-side window.

"Thank you," she whispered.

THEY REACHED NICK'S at Night in all its glory, the electric-blue neon martini glass rocking back and forth, back and forth. Hot jazz wafted out into the ocean air, along with the smells of incredible Italian cooking.

"Right this way," Sam said as he gestured up the stairs, motioning for Amanda to precede him. She had her purse and overnight case, he had two of her suitcases. Though Amanda had been here once before, she looked unsure of herself, like a leggy colt just about to bolt.

Sam knew the feeling. Sometimes, after you did

something incredibly brave, that rush of adrenaline left you high and dry. You started to cave in and wonder if you'd done the right thing after all.

He knew she had. He was positive she had. But he realized that, right now, she might not see it that way.

"Up we go," he said. "I've got to let Hercule out."

"Oh. Of course." She seemed to snap out of her daze, and swiftly started up the stairs, then down the walkway to his door.

Inside, Sam knew he had to take charge. First thing, the absolute necessities.

"Bathroom's over there. I asked Nick to bring up a cot from the storage room, so you have your choice between the sofa or the cot. We'll rig up those blankets either way."

She looked completely overwhelmed, sitting on the edge of the black leather sofa, a contented Hercule in her lap.

"Are you hungry?" Sam asked.

She nodded her head.

"I don't suppose you'd want to go down to the club and grab a bite?"

"I don't think so."

He thought of asking Nick to bring something up, but two things stopped him. One, his friend was probably in the middle of taking care of an enormous crowd of customers. And two, he had a feeling that Amanda needed to get out of this room for a while, see something different, have a change of pace.

"We can eat in the kitchen," he said. "Just the two of us and a few of the cooks."

She nodded her head.

IT WASN'T EXACTLY romantic, as first dinners went. But you couldn't beat the food, some of the best Italian cuisine in Los Angeles.

"Hey, Sam! You brought your lady friend!" Enrico, one of Nick's best cooks, tall and skinny with a black mustache and thick black hair, beamed down at the two of them.

"This reminds me," Sam muttered to Amanda as he settled them at a small table in the corner of the kitchen, "of that scene in *Lady and the Tramp.*" He laughed self-consciously. "I guess the comparison's a pretty good one."

"Sam! What have you been up to?"

Even Amanda had to smile.

"You know me, Enrico. Going after the bad guys."

"That's good, that's good. What you want?"

"What's the special?"

"Pasta à la Genovese. With pesto sauce."

Sam glanced at Amanda. She was looking around the large industrial kitchen, fascinated.

"How's that sound?"

"It's one of my favorites," she admitted.

"Two specials. And plenty of your garlic bread." He thought for a minute. "And two salads, one with Italian dressing and one with—" He glanced at Amanda.

"Blue cheese?"

"Blue cheese," he said to Enrico.

"You got it, Sam!"

He sat back in his chair. "Wine?"

She hesitated.

"On my honor, I'm on my best behavior."

"Okay."

"I'll be right back."

SAM RETURNED WITH a bottle of very decent red wine, and they dug into their salads and garlic bread as Enrico called out orders to his willing staff. In not too short a time, plates of pasta were set in front of them, the sharply aromatic scents of garlic and basil filling the air.

"This is fantastic," Amanda said, as she sampled her pasta.

"Enrico knows his way around a kitchen," Sam said.

"I do," Enrico replied as he brought them more garlic bread. "That recipe is one my mother gave to me."

They ate in a companionable silence, the sounds of jazz floating into the kitchen every time one of the waiters or waitresses opened the door and picked up an order.

"Jazz and Italian food," Sam said, sitting back a little later, his wineglass in hand. "Who would have thought it would turn out so good?"

"Nick doesn't play any music?" Amanda asked.

"Nope. He leaves that to his brother, Sonny. Nick's talents are in the kitchen. But on a night like this, with a crowd like this, he spends his time behind the bar and leaves the cooking to Enrico and the rest of the guys."

She was enjoying herself. The meal had settled quite nicely in her stomach, considering that right about now her mother would probably be getting home. But Libby might not even realize she'd left until the following morning, because if she came in late, she wouldn't stop by Amanda's bedroom and disturb her.

The amazing thing was, it felt right to be with Sam. To be sitting across this small table from him, in a restaurant kitchen, and to be talking about this and that. He was going out of his way to put her at ease, and she appreciated it.

Picking up the bottle, she poured herself another glass of wine.

Sam didn't say a word.

HE THOUGHT IT MIGHT be nice if she gave herself just a little buzz, a little glow from the wine. Just enough to fall asleep swiftly and not wake up throughout the night. Everything looked better after a good night's sleep.

She drank that last glass and her eyes drooped. Became heavy-lidded. *Bedroom eyes*, Sam thought, then hastily corrected himself.

He'd given her his word. And when Sam Cooper gave a woman his word, he stuck by it. Amanda was definitely a damsel in distress. She needed his help, not his fantasies.

"Dessert?" Enrico said, popping his head around the corner.

Sam glanced at Amanda.

"Oh, I don't think so, I'm pretty full," she replied. "But everything was...wonderful. So wonderful. Thank you."

That touched Sam. Here was a woman who had probably seen most of Europe, and experienced most of what the rich and monied did, and she was in raptures about having a plate of pesto in the back of a kitchen.

He liked that about her.

"No, I think we're done, Enrico."

"Okay. Good night, Sam. And good night to Sam's lady."

"Amanda," Sam called after him.

"Amanda. Sam, you hang on to that one." Enrico's

voice floated over from the direction of the huge restaurant-stylestove.

Sam smiled. "Another romantic," he muttered.

Amanda stood, and he noticed she touched the surface of the table lightly, to steady herself. "He's just like you, then."

It startled him, how deeply she could see beneath the surface. "Why do you say that?"

She looked up at him, her face flushed and happy. "Only a romantic would say the things you said to me the very first night we met."

"Oh. Yeah."

"Not that I'm holding you to any of that— Oh!"

He caught her elbow before she lost her balance.

"How much of that wine did you have?"

"Just a few glasses."

He supported her as they made their way out of the kitchen and into the night air. It smelled damp and heavy with sea scents. A gentle fog had rolled in, and the martini glass glowed as it blinked on into the night.

"You're never going to make the stairs," Sam said, trying to keep his tone light.

"Watch me. One foot after the other, just one foot—"

She stumbled and would have fallen if Sam hadn't caught her.

"Nope. I can't have this happen. If you fall off the steps into the parking lot, you'll wake up with some nasty bruises." His teasing tone softened the message of his words as he swung her up into his arms and started up the stairs.

"Sam." She looked up at him, and *he* almost lost his balance. What a fantasy. He thought about how it might be, bringing her home after they'd run off to Vegas and married. Carrying her over his modest threshold. Knowing they would be together for the rest of their lives.

When they reached the door, he heard scratching.

So much for fantasies. Hercule.

He nudged the door open, then carried her inside and set her down gently on the leather sofa.

"Here." He pulled the red plaid blanket from the back of the sofa and spread it over her, then grabbed a pillow and managed to maneuver it beneath her head as she slowly lowered herself to a horizontal position. "I'm just going to take Hercule out for a brief walk, then we'll be right back."

By the time he returned, she was fast asleep. Exhausted. He smiled as he looked down at her, sprawled across the couch, her head pillowed on her hand, her face finally relaxed, those tiny lines of tension gone.

Hercule whined as Sam unsnapped the leash, straining to get to the couch and his new best friend.

"Now, don't overdo it, Hercule. We have to let her rest. She's been through a lot, and—"

Of course, the French bulldog didn't listen to a single word he said. Hercule jumped up on the foot of the couch, and carefully maneuvered his way past Amanda until he'd pushed his funny little face beneath one of her arms.

"Mmm," she muttered in her sleep, pulling the dog close. "Sam."

Hercule smiled up at his master, a contented doggy grin on his face. And once more Sam found himself in the humiliating position of being jealous of his own dog.

But he had work to do. Libby would be after her

daughter very shortly. Too much was at stake. Sam had work to do, work that involved keeping Amanda safe.

"In my next life," he said softly to Hercule as he turned on his computer and settled himself behind the large, scarred desk, "I'm coming back as you."

Sam proceeded to call the best in the business, every great contact he had. Though they numbered only five, they were people he'd worked with many times before. People he could trust with his life. Contacts who would tell him the truth and work as hard for him as he would for them.

He told them the truth. About everything but the million dollars, though he implied to each of them that big money was going down. And the entire time, he made sure Amanda was deeply asleep. He didn't want her to know any of it. Or to worry.

Though how she could sleep through Hercule's little snores was beyond his comprehension.

He also had one of his best people staked out in front of the Hailey estate, and had instructed her to call if Libby made a single move.

At one in the morning, the phone rang. Sam had turned the ringer down to its lowest setting, but even then he snatched up the receiver on the first ring.

"She knows," the female voice said over the line. "She arrived home about fifteen minutes ago, then drove out again in a hurry in the beige Mercedes. I'm following her."

"Good. Not too close. There won't be that many cars in Beverly Hills this time of night."

"I'm keeping a good distance. Wherever she goes, I'll drive on by."

"Stay on the line, Emma. I don't think she's going far."

A few minutes passed, while neither said a word, though the phone line was kept open. Then—

Emma relayed an address and Sam closed his eyes.

Marvin Burgess's house. Things were happening a little more quickly than he'd expected. For some reason, he hadn't thought Libby would tell Marvin right away. The fact that she'd driven to his house this late told him all he needed to know about who was really in charge.

"Emma?"

"Yeah."

"Where are you?"

"Parked south of the estate, down the street."

"Wait there. Tell me how long she stays, and where she goes next."

"All right. Will you be up?"

"I'm not sleeping tonight." He'd gone down to the kitchen and gotten a thermos of coffee from Enrico and the crew, along with a plate of almond *biscotti*.

"I know the feeling," she said.

He smiled. "Emma? Thanks."

THE DISCREET KNOCK ON his door woke Sam from his light doze as he sat in the desk chair. It was actually an extremely comfortable chair to sleep in. He stood and stretched slowly before he walked to the door and opened it.

Nick. That meant it had to be late, because Nick wouldn't have come up until he'd put the club to bed.

"What's up?" he asked as he came inside. Then he glanced at the sofa, saw Amanda and Hercule sprawled out on it, and smiled.

"It's not what you think," Sam said.

"It's always what I think," Nick replied. "But never mind. Fill me in."

Sam did.

"So," he said, as he finished recounting the entire night's events, "I'm going to need your help. It's only a matter of time before she finds out Amanda's here."

"Sure you don't want to spend some time at the house in Maui?"

"No. I don't think we can run from this. It's got to be settled."

"I can have Mario and Phil watch the place. They could trade shifts with Luca and Michael."

"Good idea. If anyone comes around asking questions, have them play dumb and then tell me."

"You got it."

Sam pushed the plate of *biscotti* toward his friend. They'd both sat down by the desk, and now Sam reached for his coffee and took a sip. Lukewarm, but not bad.

"None for me," Nick said. "We had a very good night tonight."

"So I heard."

Nick smiled. "I'll call the guys and get them on top of it. They should be on guard within the hour."

"I appreciate it," Sam said. The men in question, bouncers for the club, were utterly loyal to Nick and his entire family. Sam knew he could trust them.

"Hey." Though Nick teased his nearest and dearest friend constantly, the expression on his face was serious. "You saved my life in Mexico. Something I'll never forget." Then he grinned. "Besides, don't you remember that old Chinese proverb? That when you save a man's life, you own him?"

Sam shook his head, trying to disguise a smile. "You've already done enough for me, Nick."

"Not nearly enough. After that week in Mexico, my dad considers you one of the family. And you know how Italians are about that sort of thing. Once you're in, you never get out."

"Thank you, Godfather."

Nick laughed softly as he got up out of his chair and headed toward the door.

SAM REMAINED AWAKE for the rest of that long night. He learned that Libby Hailey stayed at Marvin Burgess's house for two hours and twenty minutes. Long enough for Sam to get a little apprehensive. They had to be talking strategy, figuring out how to bring Amanda back into line.

And Marvin's and Libby's resources were considerable. With that sort of money, they could hire just about anyone to do just about anything.

They'd already proved to him that neither of them possessed much in the way of character. Or conscience.

At one point, just before sunrise, Sam walked to the window that overlooked the club's parking lot facing Pacific Coast Highway. He saw two dark shadowy shapes in elegant suits on the perimeter of the grounds. Apparently Mario and Phil had started their watch.

Amanda was safe.

For now.

Sam had worked as a bodyguard before. He knew his way around weapons, and had, at times, swum with such scum that he'd found himself almost in danger of becoming part of that world. Sam had seen the dark underbelly of humanity. Nothing much surprised him anymore.

But now the stakes were higher than they'd ever been. Amanda's life was on the line. Oh, he knew Libby wouldn't go as far as murder if she didn't get her way, but Sam knew exactly how much she had invested in seeing her only daughter walk down that aisle on Christmas Eve.

He sipped his coffee as he stared out at the sunrise washing the sky pale pinks and mauves. One last bright star, perhaps the planet Venus, twinkled in the night sky.

"You want a fight, Libby?" he said softly. "You've got one." Because even though Sam wasn't at all certain what was going to happen next, he was sure of one thing in a way he'd never been sure of anything before.

He would protect the woman he loved with his life.

8

LIBBY RETALIATED WITH lightning speed.

The following morning, Amanda asked Sam if he could take her shopping for a few items she'd forgotten. They stopped by a local ATM machine, and when Amanda attempted to withdraw some money from the account, she found out it had been frozen.

Sam's heart ached for her.

But she surprised him.

"It doesn't matter. I thought she might do this."

"Is it your money or hers?" Sam asked bluntly. He didn't feel uncomfortable asking her such a personal question. Perhaps that came from years of asking clients the most intimate questions.

"Mostly money I earned...a long time ago."

Sam thought of the tape of commercials he'd seen at Cindy's house, and wisely said nothing.

"It's okay. I have another account." And he watched, amazed, as she punched in another code and withdrew several hundred dollars in twenties.

"An account your mother knew nothing about, I take it."

She nodded her head.

He didn't ask, but she volunteered the information. "I started selling my watercolors about four years ago, with my teacher's help. She let me display some of my work in her gallery."

He was absolutely astounded by her creativity.

"Do you know how rare that is?" he said. "For any artist to sell her work?"

She smiled up at him. "I guess those classes finally came in handy."

THEY WENT TO SANTA MONICA Place, a mall by the ocean, and Amanda bought a couple of pairs of jeans, some sweaters and shirts, sneakers, a casual jacket, and a mountain of toys and treats for Hercule.

"And I'm taking you out to lunch today," she announced. "Anyplace you want to go."

Sam walked along beside her, his arms overflowing with various packages. She'd also used a debit card against her private account, and certainly done some serious damage to her bank balance today. But he had a feeling that this was a sort of feminine rebirth for Amanda—the new, casual clothes, so different from the sort she'd worn in Beverly Hills.

"How many of those watercolors did you manage to sell?"

She laughed, and the sound made him so happy.

"You can sell a lot of landscapes in four years."

THEY ATE AT A THAI restaurant near the Third Street Promenade. Sam ordered the garlic chicken, while Amanda chose a shrimp curry with coconut milk. Over iced coffee, they watched as people strolled by, the atmosphere at the beach very casual, very easy, even though it was only eleven days until Christmas.

He watched her as she took everything in, and knew this was a day that most likely wouldn't be repeated in the near future. Once Libby set her plans in motion, he would have to keep Amanda much more carefully hidden away. And always in sight, where he could keep an eye on her. Sam hated the thought of restraining her freedom once again, but promised himself it wouldn't be for long. Because once they were married, he would have certain rights, and could protect her even more.

Back at the nightclub, she gave Hercule his various squeak toys and rawhide treats. The bulldog was delirious over his prizes, and immediately he and Amanda got down to a rough-and-tumble game of tug-of-war with one of his toy shoes.

Sam watched them, happy, until his beeper went off. He recognized Cindy's number and dialed it immediately.

"She called me," Cindy said.

He didn't have to ask who "she" was. "Where are you calling from?"

"The pay phone at a local Starbucks." She lowered her voice. "No one followed me, and no one's around me now."

"Good girl. What happened?"

"I played super dumb, like I didn't know anything. Shocked, you know? She told me that if Amanda called, I had to call her right back, and I promised I would. But Sam, I asked her what she was going to do, and she told me she'd hired this guy to track her down."

"Did she give you a name?"

"No, I couldn't get it out of her. I think if I really pressed her for it, she would've been suspicious."

"You're right. Okay." He took a deep breath. "I'm really glad you called, Cindy. You have no idea how much of a help this is."

"Anything. Anytime. Gotta go." She hung up.

Sam hung up, too, staring at the phone as he gathered his thoughts. He made some notes on the pad of lined paper in front of him, then placed a few calls.

Within the hour, he knew who Libby had hired.

Anton Black was a detective he'd run across before. He'd never liked the man, who used rather unscrupulous and forceful methods to get his information. Anything to get the job done. Sam knew it was only a matter of time before he traced Amanda to his room above the nightclub.

Sam had already asked her never to answer the phone, to let the machine pick up, even if it sounded like Cindy on the answering machine. And, after their leisurely lunch in Santa Monica, on the drive back up to Malibu he'd told her that, for now, she had to stay close to the club. Close to him.

She'd agreed with everything he'd said.

He could see that guarding Amanda was not going to be difficult because of any actions on her part. He'd had to guard women before who hadn't agreed with anything he'd proposed, and they'd made his job a living hell. But Amanda was smart enough to realize he knew what he was doing, and was acting only in her best interests.

Now, as they were both confined to his quarters above the nightclub for the time being, Sam knew he had to gather even more information if they were going to have a fighting chance of staying ahead of Anton Black.

He decided to compile yet another file on Libby Hailey. Picking up the phone, he placed a call to Ellroy Hornsby, his premier computer consultant.

THAT SAME EVENING, as he was entering more data on Libby Hailey, and Amanda sat on the couch with Hercule watching *The Awful Truth* with Cary Grant and Irene Dunne, Sam finally broke the case on Fifi.

One of his most trusted contacts called him and told him he'd tracked the poodle to the city of Silverlake, just east of Hollywood. Fifi was living with a Mexican family, a mother and father and their seven children. The father, a teacher, had seen the poster and immediately called the phone number listed. After talking with him and deciding his story was legit, the contact had called Sam.

He called Mrs. Boswell immediately, and she was so excited she spilled her evening glass of Bordeaux all over the couch.

"Oh, my dear, I can't believe it! My little Fifi, alive and well! When can I see her?"

"I'm going to their house right now. I can pick you up on the way. If it's really Fifi, you'll have her home by tonight."

The woman was almost in tears, babbling with relief. Sam cautioned her not to get her hopes up, that they wouldn't know for sure until Mrs. Boswell identified her beloved pet.

As Sam hung up, he reviewed his options. There was no possible way that Anton Black could have worked this quickly and located Amanda. If they were careful, and if Amanda stayed close by his side, she could go along with him. He would feel safer if he knew exactly where she was.

He glanced over at the big-screen television. Amanda and Hercule had reached his pet's favorite part of the film, where husband and wife fought over who should have custody of their dog. Sam almost laughed out loud at the sight of Hercule's little black head, whipping back and forth at the same time and tempo as the celluloid dog's.

Sam didn't want to leave Amanda alone tonight. With that decided, he called Nick and asked him if he could borrow his Jeep one more time.

THE HOUSE IN SILVERLAKE was a crazy little bright pink stucco, one-story affair. Pink flamingos graced the front lawn, along with a statue of the Virgin Mary in the enclosed front porch. Colorful Chinese lanterns and little white lights were strung out back. Laughter, children's excited voices, and the most incredible culinary aromas floated into the air as Sam, Amanda and Mrs. Boswell headed toward the front door.

A young girl of about twelve answered their knock, and ushered them through the house and out onto the patio in back. Several children were seated around a picnic table on long benches, while the father and mother sat at either end, and an elderly lady with graying hair sat in a comfortable chair to one side.

The man rose, shook hands and introduced himself as Tomas Silva. "I know you want to see your dog," he said, addressing Mrs. Boswell. "As soon as my wife Angela and I saw the poster, we knew it was your Fifi."

Amanda waited, watching Mrs. Boswell, hoping against hope that the elderly lady she'd grown so fond of hadn't gotten her hopes up for nothing.

One of the children ran toward them, a white poodle in his arms. A poodle that looked exactly like Fifi did in her picture—except quite a few pounds heavier.

"Good heavens! Fifi, is that you?"

The dog yipped excitedly, her chubby body wiggling so wildly that the boy could no longer hold her. He let her down on the grass, and the white poodle flung herself at Mrs. Boswell, yipping and crying.

"Oh, Fifi!" Amanda watched as Mrs. Boswell knelt down on the grass, her glasses askew, and gathered the chubby ball of fluff into her arms. The elderly Mexican lady began to clap, and the rest of the family joined in, clapping and talking excitedly in Spanish.

Amanda slid her arm through Sam's. "What wonderful work you do," she said quietly. Mrs. Boswell was still down on the ground with her dog, who was now licking the tears off her face as the elderly lady quietly cried with relief.

He thought about the fact that business had been slow. That his partner, Evan, had basically cleaned him out. That most of his clients had lost faith in him. That at the beginning of this case, he'd believed he'd been reduced to the status of the fictional Ace Ventura. Now, seeing Mrs. Boswell reunited with her dog, he felt good. A small part of the world had gone right today, and he'd played a major part in it.

Before they knew what was happening, they were ushered toward the large picnic table, space was made, and platters of steaming corn tamales were produced. Tomas Silva handed Sam a beer, Amanda a soft drink, and Mrs. Boswell a glass of wine. Fifi stayed in her lap as everyone sat down at the table for the evening meal.

Over dinner, Fifi's saga was told.

"I saw the little dog one day while I was in Beverly Hills cleaning houses," Mrs. Silva explained. "She was searching through the garbage, looking for something to eat."

Mrs. Boswell looked horrified and hugged Fifi tighter. "Did she have her collar on?" she asked.

"No. No collar. I took her home, gave her a bath. She seemed so sad. I asked all the other women I knew who worked cleaning houses if they knew anyone who had lost a dog. No one knew anything."

"Then one day," Tomas continued, "I was picking my wife up from work and I saw one of your posters. I called the minute I got home."

"Thank you." Mrs. Boswell clutched her dog to her expansive bosom. "I cannot thank you enough." She hesitated a moment, then said, "But there's one thing I have to ask you."

Sam grinned, catching Amanda's eye. He had a feeling he knew what was coming.

"Why has she gained so much weight?"

Everyone at the table began to talk and laugh, until finally the grandmother called out, "That little one, she likes the tamales."

"Fifi, is this true?" Mrs. Boswell asked.

The poodle yipped, and everyone at the table dissolved into fits of laughter.

By the time they were ready to leave, Mrs. Boswell had decided that any woman who could make tamales like the ones she'd just enjoyed shouldn't be cleaning houses.

"So if you must refuse my offer of a generous reward," she said to the Silvas as they walked with her toward the Jeep, "I'm going to insist on setting you up in a little restaurant. All you have to do is make those tamales. I'll do the rest."

"But I want a dog," one of the littlest children said,

looking mournfully up at Fifi, snug in Mrs. Boswell's arms.

She knelt down. "And you shall have one. Would you like a poodle, just like Fifi?"

He nodded his head vigorously as Fifi licked his face.

"And so you shall have one! That's settled, then." She dabbed at her eyes with her lace handkerchief as she looked up at the entire family. "You'll never know how grateful I am for your simple kindness."

ON THE WAY HOME, Sam filled Mrs. Boswell in on what was going on, and asked her to please not tell Libby Hailey or Marvin that she had seen the two of them.

"Never talk to them, anyway," she sniffed. "But if I should be questioned by anyone, I don't know a thing. Now, by the way Sam, did you ever find that no-good partner of yours?"

"WHAT PARTNER?" AMANDA asked after they'd said good-night to Mrs. Boswell. "Did she mean Evan?"

He remembered mentioning something about his partner the first time Amanda had seen his room in Malibu.

"Yes."

"You still haven't located him?"

"Not for lack of trying. But I have a good feeling about it. Cases seem to break in waves, several at a time. My gut tells me that since Fifi was found, Evan should turn up shortly. Or at least some kind of clue."

SAM'S INSTINCTS WERE dead-on.

There was a message on his answering machine from one of his contacts. Evan had been seen in the seaside town of Puerto Vallarta, Mexico. And as Sam still had several connections in that city, finding him would be simple.

He would have to take Amanda with him. He wanted to. The problem was, any good P.I. could get ahold of airline-passenger lists. Having Amanda Hailey on record as traveling from LAX to Mexico would only make Anton Black's job of finding her that much easier.

"How would you like to go to Mexico with me?" he asked Amanda, and was delighted by the expression of utter excitement that filled her features.

"Really? I could help you find him?"

"Well, not exactly help me. You see, I know this friend who owns a hotel down there. He'd help me keep an eye on you while I went out and—"

The look she gave him told Sam what she thought of that idea. Perhaps guarding Amanda wasn't going to be the piece of cake he'd thought it would be.

"Amanda—"

"Sam, I want to help you. I don't want to think about the fact that I'm this big burden—"

"*That* you're not."

"Maybe I should just stay here with Nick."

"No, I—"

"Or Mrs. Boswell."

"Even worse."

"I won't get in the way. I just have a few ideas about the case."

Sam smiled down at her. It wouldn't hurt to indulge her. After all, it wasn't as if he thought Evan was going to come at him, guns blazing. Evan would probably take one look at him and try to run in the opposite direction.

"Okay. But I need to ask you to do one little thing."

"Fine." She eyed him expectantly.

"I'm going to ask you to travel under a false ID."

"Why?"

He sighed. It was one thing to let Amanda in on things on a need-to-know basis. It was another thing if a lack of that same knowledge made her more vulnerable. Briefly he told her about the detective her mother had hired, and his ruthless and unethical methods.

"What does she think she can do to me?" Amanda asked.

"My guess would be to kidnap you and take you home, then try and talk you into a Christmas Eve wedding."

"No."

"I know. But we've got to take every single precaution to keep you out of your mother's hands until Christmas has passed. Therefore, I'd feel a lot more comfortable if we traveled under other names."

"Okay."

THEIR FLIGHT LEFT THE following morning. Sam's contact at a travel agency in Malibu, Sandy Donovan, had found him an incredible discount on a pair of tickets that had been canceled at the last minute. The bride and groom in question had decided not to get married, and the honeymoon had been postponed—forever.

Sandy also knew what line of work Sam was in, and what that work entailed, so the false names he gave her didn't faze her a bit.

"Nick and Nora Charles," the travel agent said as she'd keyed in the necessary changes. "Is that generic enough for you, or what?"

Thank God Sandy wasn't a fan of classic romantic comedies, and didn't recognize the names of the characters in *The Thin Man* series of movies. Al Fontino, his contact in Hollywood for any kind of false papers, loved old movies, the ponies, his nightly brandy—and had a wicked sense of humor.

So Nick and Nora Charles were going on their honeymoon to Puerto Vallarta, Mexico. *But*, thought Sam as he settled himself in the first-class seat next to Amanda right before takeoff, *this time we're leaving the dog Asta at home.*

THEY HAD SETTLED IN AT a small hotel on the beach, run by a friend of Sam's. He'd met Ricardo years ago, and had no trouble telling him who he was looking for and also about the bit of trouble Amanda was in. Sam would have trusted Ricardo with his life. Besides, the chubby, round-faced, elderly man was loyal to a fault, and owed Sam big-time for having tracked down his runaway daughter several years ago.

"I will ask my people if any of them have seen this man," Ricardo said, as Sam handed him a picture of Evan. "Give me a few hours, and I'll probably have some answers for you."

Sam had also quietly given Ricardo a photo of Anton Black, Libby's hired detective, with directions to let him know immediately if he or any of his men saw Anton.

Sam and Amanda were sitting now in the hotel's shaded, oceanside bar. The roof of the outdoor bar consisted of thatched palm fronds, and the sides were open to the gentle, tropical ocean breeze. Amanda had taken only five minutes to change clothes after they'd arrived at the hotel, quickly applying sunscreen and slipping into a blue-and-white sundress and white sandals. She'd twisted her hair up on top of her head in a wonderfully artful manner, and silvery hoops graced her ears.

He couldn't stop looking at her. Staring like a lovesick, besotted groom. Well, he wouldn't have any trouble playing the part of the newlywed Nick Charles.

The entire time she'd been in their spacious bathroom changing, he'd been entertaining some pretty lustful thoughts. After all, as Nick and Nora, they were supposed to be here on their honeymoon. As time passed, Sam regretted taking the stand that he wasn't going to lay a hand on her, or take advantage of their circumstances. He knew Amanda needed a friend, but if he were honest with himself, he would admit he wanted much more than her friendship.

Now, as Ricardo left their table to greet another customer, Sam glanced at Amanda.

"How do you feel?" he asked.

"Fine." She gazed out toward the water, idly playing with the straw of her tropical drink. "Sam, it's so beautiful here."

That surprised him. "I thought you were the world traveler."

She smiled. "Mostly Europe, and just because I went to school there. And only on supervised school vacations. Field trips, that sort of thing."

"So you've never really been on just a casual trip? A family vacation?"

"No. My mother was always busy when I came home from school."

Sam knew that Libby had worked tremendously hard to get *Libby's World* off the ground. There probably hadn't been time for little things like family holidays. Not even a trip to Disneyland. He could picture Amanda as a little girl, alone in her room, daydreaming.

"So this is your first real vacation."

"Yes, it is."

"We'll have to work on it to make sure it's exciting."

"Oh, it already is," she said.

"Well, Nora," he teased, reaching for her hand, "how would you like to spend the rest of the day? I can't really do anything until I get some sort of lead. The one bringing us down here was pretty vague, but it felt right."

"I'd like to talk about Evan."

He frowned. This wasn't what he'd had in mind.

"Evan?"

"Your partner."

"I know that. What do you want to talk about?"

She leaned forward, all her attention centered on him, and, not for the first time, Sam thought about what an incredible listener she was.

"Tell me about him."

HE SPENT THE NEXT HOUR doing exactly that. Explaining how he and Evan had met, in Baltimore, at an evening adult-education course on changing your career path. Evan had been working at a bank, Sam in construction. Both of them had known they wanted something different out of life. Something more.

They'd enjoyed that class. Had gone regularly to a nearby bar and talked afterward, along with other classmates. Had enjoyed each other's take on life, sense of humor.

The final class had been something of a career day. And one of the people there had been Joseph Krobot, a private detective and a brilliant and fascinating speaker. Sam and Evan had been hooked. They'd both gone to work for him, learning the business in the best way possible—with a real pro.

Four years later, Joe retired and moved with his wife, Celeste, to Florida. Sam and Evan had continued the business, until Evan's mother's failing health had made them consider moving to a warmer climate. Sam had always loved the beach life anyway, and so they'd relocated to southern California. Newport Beach.

The tenor of their cases changed. Newport Beach offered them plenty of rich clients: cheating husbands, embezzling businessmen, rebellious and runaway teenagers. Their business expanded. They became more successful, more affluent, putting more money back into the business and buying more sophisticated computer equipment. Moving to a snazzier office. Maintaining a growing base of contacts and clients.

Then, the unthinkable. Evan hadn't come into work for a few days. No one answered the phone when Sam called his residence. When he went to his friend's luxury apartment, the landlady informed Sam that Evan had cleaned the place out and left.

After checking the company bank account, Sam had realized what Evan had done to him. They hadn't been wealthy, but the business had been in the black.

"The thing I don't understand," he said to Amanda, who had been listening carefully the entire time, "is that it was so unlike Evan. I never thought—he didn't seem the type of man who would do that."

"So you lost faith in your own judgment," she said softly.

"Yeah. Big-time." He took another long swallow of his chilled Corona.

"Sam, Evan didn't have a girlfriend, a wife, a child from a previous marriage? Someone he loved, someone who would know where he was?"

"Nope. He was the perennial bachelor. The only family he had was his mom, and she was one great lady."

"She passed away?"

"No. As far as I know, she's still alive. But I lost touch with her, and even if I had known where she was, I couldn't have brought myself to tell her that her son had basically committed a criminal act."

Amanda appeared to be considering all of this as she looked out at the waves, rhythmically beating against the white sand. A gentle ocean breeze ruffled the palm fronds of the trees near the shoreline, the sound a gentle tick-tick-tick.

"Sam, I don't think your judgment failed you at all. But I think you've overlooked the obvious."

"Such as?" He wasn't at all offended by what she said. Perhaps Amanda, an outsider taking a fresh look at this particular case, could give him some insight.

"You've known Evan for years. In all that time, he never betrayed you. Suddenly he leaves and cleans out the agency's bank account. That doesn't sound like the work of a con man. It sounds like the behavior of a desperate man."

"I know. I used to lie awake at night and wonder how Evan could have done it."

"He had to be very frightened, Sam. Wouldn't you agree?"

He hadn't looked at it from that viewpoint. He'd simply been devastated by his business partner's betrayal. Now he realized he'd been too close to see the obvious.

Sometimes all you needed was fresh input.

"So you're saying—"

"Who did he love, Sam? You said it yourself. The two of you moved to a warmer climate because his mother was having trouble with her health."

He nodded his head, thinking ahead, believing he could see where she was heading with this.

"Did she ever get better?"

"No. Her health was always kind of iffy."

"Did your business offer the two of you medical insurance? Did Evan's mother have medical coverage?"

"Not with us. Because—" Sudden comprehension dawned. "Evan tried to get her coverage. I remember they wouldn't take her on at a decent rate because she had what they considered a preexisting condition."

Amanda leaned forward, her eyes bright, pushing her drink out of the way. "Did he seem worried for a few weeks before he disappeared?"

"He was...nervous. I asked him a couple of times if he thought he was burning out, needed a rest. He took a week in—" He stared at her. "Mexico."

"Bingo," she said softly.

"He was setting the whole thing up even then," Sam said slowly. He studied Amanda. "What made you make the connection to his mother?"

"Maria, our housekeeper, is from Mexico City. We used to talk all the time when I was home on vacation. She used to tell me all about her country. I remember one conversation about how a lot of rich people came to

Mexico when they were ill for alternative treatments they couldn't get in the United States."

"His mother," Sam said gently. "Of course."

"If he took the money because his mother needed it for some kind of medical treatment," Amanda said, "he must have been desperate. You can't just run into him and start yelling at him."

Sam stared at her. He'd faced down vicious thugs in dark alleyways. Moved among the Los Angeles and Newport Beach underworlds. Consorted with criminals in order to get that choice bit of information that might shed some light on a particularly difficult case.

Now this young woman, this ethereal blonde, was telling him, totally unafraid, that he couldn't just run off and punch Evan in the jaw the way he'd been fantasizing about for months. Sometimes that particularly satisfying daydream had been all that had kept him going.

"I can't, huh?" Her intensity touched him more than he wanted to admit.

"No. You can't. He's your friend and your partner. Your judgment of people is rock solid. Evan wasn't, and isn't a bad man. Just a desperate one, who made a serious error in judgment."

Sam glanced up as he saw Ricardo heading toward their table, a grin on his lined, tanned face.

Something was up.

The older man joined them.

"One of my men has seen him. Always at the same place, every day. Up in the mountains, by a private house. He thinks it's some kind of clinic."

Sam glanced at Amanda. Met her gaze. She smiled.

"What time?"

"He's there at about noon. If you want, I can have my man take you there tomorrow afternoon."

"I'd like to go, too," Amanda said.

Sam opened his mouth on an automatic refusal, then saw the strong resolve in those gentle blue eyes. And he knew that Amanda wanted to be there to make sure there was a certain degree of civility to his meeting with Evan.

He had a feeling he wouldn't be able to talk her out of it. Besides, logic and instinct told him she would be safer with him.

"All right." He glanced at Ricardo. "Tomorrow we'll meet your man here at, what? Eleven?"

"Eleven is fine. He can use my car, and take the two of you." Ricardo smiled at both of them. "In the meantime, I would suggest taking advantage of our beautiful beaches. I can offer you the use of my boat if you'd like to do a little exploring on your own."

Sam glanced at Amanda. He'd exhausted most of his contacts. Ricardo had beaten the bushes and his men had brought out the necessary information. He and Amanda really couldn't do anything until the following day, so there was no reason they just couldn't enjoy themselves.

"I'd like to get some sun," Amanda said. "Maybe a swim."

Sam nodded. The thought of seeing Amanda in a bathing suit brought a slow, satisfied smile to his face. Perhaps they would accomplish more on this trip than finding out exactly what had happened to his business partner.

The thought brought him enormous pleasure.

9

AMANDA HAD LOOKED AT Puerto Vallarta with an artist's eye from the moment she and Sam had arrived. She'd never been to Mexico before, and this city, which had once been a small, remote, Indian fishing village, charmed her.

There were the obvious attractions. The blue Pacific, the palm trees rustling in the ocean breezes, the impossibly white sand and bright sunshine. But it was also the fact that the town was surrounded by mountains and tropical jungle. Those jungle cliffs came straight down to the white-sand beaches, creating a dramatic view.

And the color. She reveled in the brilliant flowers spilling over patio walls, and the lush, tropical gardens. Her fingers itched to sketch the white houses with their red tile roofs, perched on the hillsides.

Ricardo's hotel, with its incredible view of the bay, was one of the smaller, more intimate hotels along the beach. Quiet and tucked away, it was the sort of place romantic getaways and honeymoons were made of.

But she wasn't here on a honeymoon. She was here to help Sam find his ex-partner. Actually, she thought as she pulled on her swimsuit, she wasn't even here to do that. She was here because he couldn't afford to leave her in Malibu, what with this Anton Black after her. Sam had taken her on as yet another responsibility, and Amanda didn't like the feeling that gave her.

She wanted to be a partner. Not a responsibility. Not a burden. Her mother had told her repeatedly, over the years, what it had cost her financially and emotionally to raise her to adulthood. The sacrifices she had made.

Now, having left her mother's mansion, Amanda was determined to make her own way in the world once Christmas Eve passed and there was absolutely no possibility of her marrying Marvin. The watercolors she'd sold had been just the start.

She also had to figure out what part Sam was going to play in her life. Because she couldn't see just walking away from him when all of this was over. Yet she had to make sure he wasn't the sort of person who was going to try to organize her life for her. Decide what she could or could not do. In her heart, she couldn't believe he would attempt that sort of thing, but her newfound freedom was so precious to her, she found herself wanting to protect it, nurture it, allow it to bloom.

Finished with applying a generous layer of sunscreen, she reached for her discarded clothing and opened the bathroom door.

HER SUIT PRACTICALLY gave him a coronary.

"You're going out in that?"

"In what?"

"That...that..." He gestured to the minuscule suit she wore, which, in his opinion, barely covered the essentials. Who would have thought that Amanda, his shy princess from Beverly Hills, would even consider wearing something like...that?

The bikini was a tropical pattern of turquoise and white, with floral blooms and palm fronds running riot over two triangles of fabric barely covering her breasts,

and an extremely abbreviated bottom. When she turned
to pick up her sandals, Sam swallowed.

"What?" She glanced back at him.

"That...that..."

"This?" She indicated the swimsuit bottom. "Oh, I
know. It's a little briefer than a regular bikini bottom,
but not quite a thong. Don't worry, I made sure I applied plenty of sunscreen."

That thought sent his imagination into overdrive.

"Ah...I'll just be a minute," Sam said. "Put on my
suit, that sort of thing."

"Okay. I'll wait." She picked up the television remote
and clicked on a channel as Sam made a hasty exit.

She watched him retreat into the bathroom, then
couldn't repress a smile.

She loved him. She'd discovered she loved Sam when
he'd driven her back to the club the night she'd run
away. She'd loved him when he'd made his declaration
that he wasn't going to take advantage of the situation,
or her. She loved him, because even though it was the
late twentieth century and they were on the coast of
Mexico, Sam was her knight in shining armor.

He had a certain moral code. He believed in behaving
with honor. He was a chivalrous man.

And that made all the difference.

Now all she had to do was convince him that it was
okay to take advantage of her. Because she knew, without a doubt, that he was the one.

THE LATE-AFTERNOON sunshine wasn't as blindingly hot
as it had been earlier. They sat beneath an umbrella,
shielded from the worst of the sun's rays, and ordered
two tall glasses of a tropical fruit-juice blend. Then they

lay back on the large beach towels the hotel had provided and simply relaxed.

Sam, propped on one elbow, watched the tumbling surf. He didn't dare look at Amanda. He was going crazy, lying next to her, both of them practically naked in their suits. The combination of hot sun, tropical breezes, the relaxed atmosphere, the highly charged tension that seemed to grip him every time he was near her, the—

"Sam?" She was gazing up at him as she lay stretched out on the towel beside him.

"Hmm?" She looked heartbreakingly beautiful to him. That golden hair, those long-lashed, brilliant blue eyes—

"I want you to make love to me."

His heart slammed to a complete stop.

"I WANT YOU TO MAKE love to me."

The words had hummed in his ears as he'd stared at her.

I want you to make love to me.

He'd gotten slowly to his feet, taken her hand as she stood, steadied her as she lost her balance in the soft sand. Then they'd grabbed their towels, their drinks.

I want you to make love to me....

By the time they'd reached the steps of their hotel, he'd set his half-empty glass down on one of the nearby tables and swung her up into his arms.

Now, as he unlocked their hotel-room door, still carrying her, and walked inside, Sam's knees felt shaky.

He set her down on the side of one of the large, queen-size beds. Their room hadn't even been slept in yet; the bed still looked pristine and fresh. He'd just been given his heart's desire, and he was nervous in a way he hadn't been since high school.

Because it meant so much. No, because *she* meant so much. He wanted what was going to happen to be a memory they would both cherish for the rest of their lives.

And because he hadn't seen this coming. Oh, he'd wanted it, but he'd thought it might happen after they returned to L.A. After Christmas Eve, and the time limit for that awful wedding had passed. After everything with Evan had been put to rest.

Not now, not at this moment, not right now...

Sam wanted this so badly, but he had to make sure. Carefully, he knelt down beside her, his knees on the carpet, and took her hand.

"Amanda."

She looked at him, their eyes met.

"This isn't just because of sun and ocean breezes and the fact that we're in an incredibly romantic place?"

"No, Sam," she said. "No."

"Okay."

"Can I ask a favor?" she whispered.

"Anything."

"Could you pull the drapes shut?"

He understood. Amanda surely didn't have so much experience that she would want to make love in broad daylight. Though he would have loved it, would have loved to see the sunshine dance over every single curve of her body. He rose to get the drapes and as he was sliding them shut, a thought crossed his mind.

"Amanda?" he said as he headed back toward the bed where she still sat. Not that he'd expected her to start executing an intricate striptease. In fact, if his suspicions were correct—

"Have you ever done this before?"

She hesitated, and he had her answer before the words were out of her mouth. "Well, there was this one boy in Switzerland I really liked, and then this tennis instructor, but I—"

She was babbling and he knew it. He took her hand, pulled her back against the soft bedspread.

"But did you ever ask them to make love to you?"

Her breath caught in a peculiar little hitch that tore at his heart. Then she said, "No," and he noticed her voice had gone up a few tones. Nervous. She was nervous.

Probably because it meant so much. Hopefully because *he* meant so much.

"Amanda," he said, deliberately only touching her hand. If he touched any other part of her practically naked body, he wouldn't be able to exert much control over his basic thought processes. "I want to know."

"Why?"

"It makes a difference."

"You don't think I'm...strange?"

Ahh. That's it.

"Not at all. Just that you have extremely good taste. As I do."

She started to laugh in the darkened bedroom, and he smiled.

"After all, you could have had anyone. Anyone at all. I'm just making sure you want to throw it all away on a guy like me."

"Sam." She turned toward him now, and in the muted light he could see the smile on her face. "I think you're very special."

He kissed her hand. "I can't begin to tell you what this means to me," he said. "And I want you to know that I'm not going to try and run your life for you. That's your job."

"Thank you," she whispered.

HE'D NEVER BEEN WITH a virgin before, so Sam decided he was going to have to wing it. The one thing he was sure of was that he wanted to make this special.

"I've got some sand on my legs," he said. "Would you mind if I took a quick shower?"

She nodded, with such relief that he realized she needed some time alone. She'd probably made this decision on the spur of the moment, and now needed a few minutes to reflect on what she was about to do. Because once they started, there would be no turning back.

He headed into the shower, turned on the strong spray, stepped inside. Rinsed off the sand, lathered off the tanning lotion. Ducked his head beneath the spray and even shampooed his hair. Got out, toweled off, brushed his teeth.

When he entered the bedroom, he realized he'd half expected her to bolt. Instead, she headed into the bathroom and he heard her turn on the shower.

Smiling, he placed a call downstairs.

SHE SPENT A LONG TIME in the steam-filled bathroom, pondering the next step she was about to take.

It felt right. Even if Sam never offered her anything in the way of a future, it felt right. Amanda realized that, no matter what happened, she wouldn't regret asking

Sam to be the man who would introduce her to intimacy.

She stepped out of the shower. Toweled off. Blew her hair dry and brushed her teeth. Wrapped one of the pale peach bath sheets around her naked body, and finally admitted to herself that she was stalling a little because she was scared.

She couldn't stall any longer.

So excited and scared and intimidated that her stomach fluttered and her hands shook slightly, Amanda stepped out of the bathroom.

He'd pulled the bedspread off the bed so just the sheets remained. Sam was lying in bed, and she was grateful for the fact that he'd drawn the top sheet up to his waist. His chest looked strong and muscular, dusted with dark hair. She'd never noticed how big the muscles in his arms were. She hesitated, suddenly aware of just how alone they were.

The knock on the door startled her.

"I'll get it." Sam left the bed, quickly grabbed a toweling robe, and approached the door. She heard him exchange a few words with a waiter, then she watched as Sam wheeled a room-service cart inside.

"Champagne," he said quietly. "You should always have champagne your first time." He expertly uncorked the bottle, filled two flutes, and handed her one.

"To a night," he said, "that neither of us will forget."

Her eyes filled as she took the champagne flute from him. He understood. Everything was going to be all right.

They each drank a glass of champagne before Sam got down to business. Taking off his robe, he quickly slid beneath the sheet, then patted the bed beside him.

She felt like joining him, but wasn't sure if she would feel comfortable naked in front of him just yet. A horrible sense of modesty washed over her. It was the strangest thing, because she knew she wanted to make love with Sam. She just wasn't sure that she wanted him to see her naked. Not just yet.

She knew it made absolutely no sense. She'd worn the most abbreviated of swimsuits on the beach just now, but she couldn't drop her towel and stand in front of him. Even though she knew it was exactly what he wanted.

She hesitated.

He understood.

"I'll just look the other way," he said.

Grateful, she dropped the towel and slid into bed.

"I'm sorry the room's not a little darker," he whispered as he took her into his arms. "I suppose you could blindfold me—"

She started to laugh then, because suddenly it was all right. The minute he'd touched her, it was all right.

"No," she said, just before he kissed her. "It's going to be fine."

He wanted more than fine. He wanted over the moon. And Sam knew he would give this woman anything she wanted. If she wanted him to stand on his head and whistle Dixie before she would get in the mood, then he would just pucker up his lips and blow.

Now, all he knew was that she'd offered him an incredible gift. Not just her virginity, but the trust that went with it. The trust that would enable him to be the one to introduce her to lovemaking.

He kissed her. She tasted of fine champagne and

some kind of peach scent. Probably her bath gel or soap. He didn't care, he was so hungry for her. It took every bit of control he could muster not to just push her over on her back, open her legs and slide right in.

Instead, he kissed her. Kissed her again. Kissed her until she was grasping his shoulders and breathing with an urgency that matched his. Only then did he reach down and cup one of her breasts in his hand. The firm flesh felt hot against his palm, the nipple so hard. He rolled it gently between his thumb and forefinger, smiling against her mouth as he heard the sound of her stunned pleasure in the quick intake of her breath, then the sweetest of moans.

Sliding down the softness of her body, he took the nipple into his mouth, pulled on it. Felt himself grow even harder, if that was possible. He wished she would put her hands on him, then his body jerked in surprise when she did. Her fingers were tentative at first, then touched him more strongly, exploring.

He broke contact with her breast, gritting his teeth against the almost overpowering sensation. He knew she had to feel him, explore him, know what it was that would be going inside her body. But the sensation of those smooth fingers against his hotly aroused flesh was nearly too much.

He groaned, then smothered the sound against her mouth as he took it in another long kiss. He covered her hand with his own and stilled all movement, knowing that if she continued to arouse him this way, their evening might be over sooner than they thought.

"Please, Sam," she whispered, her lips against his

ear, and he realized she didn't want to wait any longer. She wanted to know.

He slid his hand down, found her, opened her and touched her, hot and wet. More than ready. But he knew he couldn't possibly just plunge ahead. He had to take control of the situation, because he knew what she wanted. He'd built her to a plateau of sensation, and she needed release.

She moaned as he slid a finger inside her, found her again, began to stroke her. She clutched at him, her body pressing against him, then she put a hand over his own and pressed it hard, hard, right there—

And she came.

Overwhelmed by that exquisite sensitivity, he kissed her cheeks, her forehead, her eyelids, her mouth.

"Sam," she murmured, as if coming out of a dream. "Sam."

He held her tightly against him, caressing her in long strokes from her neck to the backs of her thighs. And he suddenly wondered if her mother had told her anything. Or if she'd even needed to, in this day and age.

He had to say something.

"This may hurt a little," he whispered in her ear.

"I don't care," she whispered back, and he smiled, so happy to hear that fire and spirit.

She ran her fingers through his hair as she kissed him, and Sam suddenly knew he had to say it, had to let her know before he took her in the most intimate way possible.

"Amanda," he said, his lips brushing her ear, "I love you. I love you. And it's not just because—"

She stopped his declaration with a kiss. When they both came up for air, she said, "I know. Me, too."

"I want you, and I love you, and I had to let you know." He slid up over her, eased her thighs apart. She looked up at him, and he could see the little bit of apprehension in her eyes.

"I love you," he whispered.

That seemed to relax her.

Then he couldn't talk anymore as he positioned himself against her, then pushed. Slowly. Carefully. Slid inside, filling her, reaching the barrier and knowing there was no way around it, that it had to be breached.

His eyes held hers as he pushed. As she gave way to him, to his absolute possession of her. There was no other way it could be, but as he slid fully inside her, he heard a sharp little cry and stopped. Levered his body up on his elbows. Looked down at her.

She was crying.

"Oh, God. Did I hurt—"

In answer, she encircled his hips with her legs, pulling him all the way inside.

"No. No, keep going, please! It's just... It's just..."

He knew what she meant.

It was beautiful.

AFTERWARD, AFTER AN orgasm that he was sure had fried neurons in his brain, Sam mumbled into the pillow, "I had condoms with me. I just forgot."

She simply laughed.

He raised his head, opened an eye. "Young lady, in this day and age, that's not very funny."

"Yes, it is," she gasped, between laughs. "Because I had some, too. In my purse."

"You did?" This surprised him.

She nodded her head.

"Amanda. You never cease to amaze me. When did you start carrying them?"

"After the French film. I bought some the next day."

Well, I'll be damned.

"Really."

She nodded her head.

"You were thinking about me in that way, at that time?"

"Yes."

"Why didn't you let me know?" he asked.

"I still wasn't completely sure."

"How sure were you?"

"About eighty percent."

"What tipped you over the edge?" He had to know. It was probably because he'd had the sensitivity to sit through a film like that, and all for her.

"I liked the way you smiled."

If he lived to be a hundred, he would never be able to fathom the way women thought.

"Hmm." He considered this. Then realized he had to consider something else.

"Do you know where you are in your cycle?"

She told him.

"You could be pregnant," he said, taking this thought in at the same time he said it.

"I know."

"Does that upset you?"

She hesitated. "No."

The minute she said the words, he knew they were true for him.

"I want you to know, that if you are, well, what I want you to know is that—"

I'll be there for you.

Hell, those weren't the words he wanted to say. But he was scared to death to say the others. After all, what did he really have to offer a woman like Amanda?

But he had no other choice. Sam jumped off the end of the proverbial pier, into deep water.

"Pregnant or not, I love you, and I want to—what I mean is—will you marry me?"

Those blue eyes. So clear. So sure. Not a single second's hesitation, and he loved her for it.

"Yes." Within a heartbeat, she was in his arms.

After kissing her senseless, Sam remembered. A ring. Usually, when a man asked a woman to marry him, he presented her with an engagement ring.

Marvin had given her a diamond of several karats. Many karats. It had sparkled on her finger like a small sun when she'd danced with him at the engagement party. Amanda had given the impressive piece of jewelry to Cindy, in its original velvet box, with instructions to have it messengered to Marvin's office immediately—no return address. Just to make sure he got it and knew in no uncertain terms that their wedding was off.

While he, suave and debonair Sam, had just asked the most beautiful woman in the world to be his bride, and had no ring.

His eye caught the champagne bottle. The foil on the neck glinted.

It would have to do.

"Just a minute," he said, releasing his brand-new fiancée and reaching for the bottle. He tore off several strips of the silvery foil and crushed them together, forming a crude ring.

"Amanda—"

"Oh, Sam—"

"I wish they could be diamonds," he said, fitting the foil ring around her finger. "I wish I had a million diamonds I could give you. I wish I could cover your body with them—"

She was crying now, and, knowing Amanda as he did, Sam took this as a good sign.

"Someday," he said as he kissed her, "they will be. Do you believe that?"

She nodded her head, then turned on the bedside lamp and held her hand up to it, letting the foil glint in the light.

"Sam?"

"Yeah?" He'd never felt as vulnerable in his life.

"It's the most beautiful ring I've ever seen."

He opened his mouth to protest and she stopped him with a look.

"Can't you see the diamonds? Right there, and there, and...there."

If it was at all possible, he fell in love with her even more.

"I...I think I do," he said, his voice rough.

"Of course you do," she replied, her voice breaking, tears sheening her eyes. "Their light is just filling this entire room. You can see them, Sam, can't you?"

He knew what she was telling him. In her own way,

she had utter faith in him. She would hitch her fortune with his, for better or worse. And right now, he was definitely in the "worse" phase of his career.

His chest swelled, emotion tightened his throat. Taking her hand, he pulled her down on the bed beside him.

"I do," he whispered. Then he kissed her, running his fingers through her silken hair. "I do."

10

IT TURNED OUT TO BE a sort of honeymoon after all.

They stayed in their room for the remainder of the day, ordering up a platter of nachos and margaritas. Made love again, this time much more slowly and with considerable tenderness. A true consummation of everything they felt.

Just before sunset, Sam took Amanda to Chez Elena, which he considered the most romantic restaurant in Puerto Vallarta. It was located on a hill, overlooking the city.

They went to the roof garden for drinks and a view of the spectacular sunset, then inside for dinner. Strolling singers moved among the tables, words of love in their songs. Sam couldn't get through their dinner without holding Amanda's hand, touching her cheek, giving her quick kisses. He still couldn't quite believe she'd agreed to marry him.

And he realized that his mother had, as always, been right. When you met the right person, it was easy. Things fell into place. Love wasn't supposed to be hard, or full of doubt. When it was right, it was right.

They walked along the shoreline when they returned to the hotel, then retired early. And Sam thought, as he stood on their balcony with his arms around Amanda and looked out over the darkness of the bay and the twinkling stars dotting the sky, that if they'd anticipated their honeymoon just a little, that was all right with him.

THE FOLLOWING MORNING, at eleven, they met Ricardo and one of his men, Louis, at the bar.

"Louis will take you to the place he sees this man," Ricardo said. "From there, we will leave it up to you, Sam."

"He's there every single day?" Sam asked, directing his question to Louis. The man was tall and lean, his face tanned and lined, his hair a gray stubble.

"Every day. I think he visits someone. He looks uneasy."

As he damn well should, Sam thought. "Okay. Let's go."

THE AREA OF THE CITY Louis had brought them to was a hillside neighborhood, filled with quiet streets and alleyways. A total contrast to the bustling beachfront, which teemed with activity, it was a residential area that didn't cater to the tourist trade.

Louis had parked the car and directed both Sam and Amanda to a local café. They all ordered coffee, then situated themselves at a corner table that was tucked away behind a few others but still offered an excellent view of the street.

Sam was on his second cup of coffee, and a pastry, when he spotted his former partner walking briskly down the street. Sam's eyes narrowed. Evan had usually been the cockier of the two of them, ready to take on the world. Ready to at least present that facade even if he didn't feel that way.

This man bore no resemblance to his ex-partner.

"There he is," Louis said, his voice low. "Let me know if you need my help."

"We shouldn't," Sam replied, still watching Evan.

Amanda laid a hand on his arm. "Don't scare him, Sam. He looks like he'd run at the slightest provocation."

"I know." Sam continued to watch his partner as he walked along the cobblestone street. "I think I'm going to tail him. See where he's going. What he's up to."

"An excellent idea," Louis said under his breath. "You see that building up ahead? He always goes inside. Every day."

"You see a lot," Sam remarked.

Louis nodded, and Sam sensed this was all he was going to get out of the man.

EVAN LEFT THE STUCCO building almost exactly an hour after he entered it. His spirits seemed better, he walked with a little more spring in his step. This time, Sam slowly got out of his chair, intending to follow his ex-partner.

"Louis, would you watch Amanda?" he asked, before he left the table.

"Of course."

Amanda didn't bristle, as she knew he was only concerned for her safety. So far, no one in the vicinity had seen the detective Anton Black, but she'd agreed with Sam that they couldn't be too careful.

She watched as Sam fell into step behind Evan. The two men continued up the road until they were out of sight, Sam tailing Evan closely while never letting the man get a feeling that he was being followed.

Amanda observed the way he worked, amazed. Sam

walked slowly but carefully, using doorways, cars, even other people to conceal himself. Yet he never appeared obvious.

As soon as the two men had left the area, she turned to Louis. "Would you mind if we did some investigating of our own?"

He took a sip of his coffee, set it down. "What did you have in mind, *señorita*?"

"I'd like to see exactly what's inside that building."

WHEN SAM REJOINED Louis and Amanda at the café, he had a discouraged expression on his face.

"He saw me." he said, with no preamble as he sat down at the table. "He saw me, I spooked him, and he ran."

Louis grimaced. "Now that he knows you're in town, he will be a lot more careful."

"He'll be back," said Amanda.

Sam turned his attention toward her. "How can you be so sure of that?"

"Because that building he was inside for an hour today? It's a medical clinic that specializes in specific alternative medical treatments," she said.

Amanda had ordered lunch for them, and as they sat in the shade enjoying grilled fish, guacamole, and rice and beans, she continued to explain what she and Louis had learned.

"I told the man in charge that my father was ill, and I was getting discouraged with conventional medical treatment in the States. Louis posed as my husband. I asked the director if I could speak with a few of the more elderly patients, and see if they were happy with the treatment they were receiving before asking my elderly father to make such a drastic move."

"And?" Sam prompted. He couldn't get over all she'd done while he'd been tailing Evan.

"I talked with a Mrs. Cynthia Steiger."

"Evan's mother," Sam said. "I'll be damned."

"Sam, she has cancer, but her treatment is progressing wonderfully and the outlook is good. She loves the clinic, and she talked about you and Evan. She's so proud of you both. As far as she knows, Evan is still in business with you in Newport Beach. She thinks Evan has only taken an extended leave of absence."

Sam put down his fork, stunned. He stared at her, amazed.

"Now, Louis posed as my husband, so we gave the impression of a married couple looking for a place for my father. I also talked to some of the working staff, including the janitor—"

"The janitor speaks English?" Sam interrupted.

"No. I speak Spanish."

"Fluently," Louis added. "You should have heard her."

Sam sat back in his chair, not sure how many more surprises he could take in today.

"There's a huge charity party being given tonight. Up in one of the homes on the hillside. Anyway, the director of the clinic extended an invitation to me and my husband—" she glanced at Louis as she said this "—and I managed to ask if we could bring along one of our friends from the area."

"Me," Sam said, not at all sure he liked the idea of Louis posing as Amanda's husband. Irrational, yes. Jealous, yes. A man in love—again, yes.

"Right. So, now all we have to do is show up at that party tonight and make sure you manage to talk to Evan before he sees you and runs."

"Right," Sam said, staring down at his grilled fish. This case had jumped right out of his hands at some point. He'd walked away, tailing Evan, and when he'd come back, Amanda had not only gathered a lot of new information, but had their entire evening's agenda mapped out.

"You could always say that I was tired," Louis offered. "I stayed back in the room, being the old man that I am." His dark eyes twinkled in his lined face. "But my lovely young wife, well, she wanted to go to a party, and I am secure enough in my marriage to trust my dear friend to take her to this party."

Sam opened his mouth. Shut it. Louis was behaving in an incredibly generous way, and he was being a jerk. There was no way around it. It was way past time to swallow his pride and be gracious.

"I—thank you, Louis. That's an excellent idea. And Amanda, I can't thank you enough for getting all that information. I think we have a fighting chance of finding Evan again and trying to talk to him."

"Oh, you don't have to thank me," she replied, enthusiasm shining in her expression. "It was fun."

Sam picked up his fork, toyed with his fish, then covertly stared at the woman across from him. It was as if she'd suddenly grown another head. Who would have thought that Amanda Hailey would be a natural in the world of private detectives? Fluent in Spanish, clever with the improvisations, sincere, logical and smart in her approach.

And this was not good, because the last thing he

wanted was to ever put her in a position where she might be hurt.

Good Lord, I've created a monster.

THEY BORROWED RICARDO'S car once again, and that evening made their way up the precarious hillside road. The head of the private clinic had assured them that dress would be very casual for this event, as Puerto Vallarta was a casual sort of town. The object of tonight's gathering was to have fun and raise money. Most of the wealthy locals had come down to this area in the first place in order to kick back. Casual slacks, colorful shirts and informal dresses were the order of the day.

"What name did you use back at the clinic?" Sam asked as he carefully maneuvered Ricardo's big Cadillac around a pickup truck carrying what looked like an entire family, including several chickens and two pigs. He hoped she hadn't used her real name. It was more information that Anton Black could find and use.

"Oh, not my own," she said. "I told the director we were Hercule and Fifi Boswell."

"Fifi? You called yourself Fifi and he bought it?" He felt incredulous, and a little annoyed. She was too good. One of those naturals who fell into this line of work as if they were born to it.

"Well, of course. I mean, I can speak French fluently."

"And Spanish," Sam said, trying not to sound petty. "Any others I should know about?"

"German and Italian. Oh, and just a smattering of Chinese," she replied matter-of-factly.

Sam glanced over at her to make sure she wasn't joking. "You're not kidding, are you?"

"I minored in languages."

He couldn't bring himself to ask her what she'd really focused on in school, so he merely concentrated on the road as the large car headed up the hill.

Before they reached the party, it started to rain.

"This is not good," Sam muttered.

"Because of your disguise?" Amanda asked.

Before they'd left the hotel, he'd remade his face. Some spirit gum applied around the nose, another set of false teeth, a mustache, a goatee and thick-lensed tortoiseshell glasses. He'd planned to look like a nerd, the furthest thing from what he actually was. The last thing he wanted Evan to do was cut and run. His partner would definitely be there tonight, as he was helping chair the auction that would raise money for the clinic. Sam wanted to make sure he had a chance to talk to him.

"Yeah. The last thing I need is to lose the mustache in this downpour."

"I could drive you up to the entrance, then park the car," Amanda suggested. "We could switch places."

"No, not a good idea. There's going to be a lot of mud around this house by the time we get there. I'll have to try and find a dry place. But I can let you out by the door."

She opened her mouth to disagree with him, then reconsidered. Sam had been a little testy since this morning, and she'd assumed it was because Evan had seen him and run. She knew how important it was for Sam to make contact with his ex-partner, so now she pressed her lips together and said nothing. He had enough on his mind.

Some of the houses perched on the hillside were truly spectacular, with their views of the tropical jungle, the mountains and the Pacific Ocean. Generous balconies ran the length of these mansions, and windows gleamed with light against the swiftly darkening sky. Rain pelted down on the car's windshield, which had been so dusty that the first few swipes of the wiper blades had reduced their visibility to a smeared mess.

Now it was slanting down in sheets—a highly unusual occurrence because December wasn't considered part of this region's rainy season. But, she thought, weather patterns had been unpredictable for the past few years, so why would Mexico be any different?

"Here we are," Sam announced, guiding the big luxury car through the rain. Amanda glanced ahead at the enormous house directly in front of them. She covertly eyed Sam, then decided to let him run things for the time being.

He dropped her off at the main entrance, promising to join her as soon as possible.

She walked up the broad steps, accepted a glass of tropical punch from a casually dressed waiter on the large stone terrace, then entered the main room. Though the place was packed to capacity, she recognized Evan immediately. He was talking to an elderly man, his expression animated. She smiled, thinking about Evan's mother and what a relief her improving health must be to him.

She sipped her punch, waiting for Sam to join her. He'd promised to be only a few minutes, and when almost ten had passed and he hadn't arrived, she walked toward one of the large windows and glanced outside.

The grounds were beautifully landscaped, tropical plants all around, flowers blooming riotously. Yellow and red hibiscus, salmon-colored bougainvillea, and a few others she couldn't readily identify. Again, her artist's fingers itched to draw them, capture their beauty on her sketchbook. The colors looked so fresh and vibrant after the brief, hard rain. The air coming in the window smelled wonderfully sweet, moist and alive with growing things.

But where was Sam?

A MAN IN CASUAL SLACKS and a brightly patterned Hawaiian shirt had directed Sam to a certain spot with a wave of his hand, but as Sam had attempted to park Ricardo's big boat of a car, he'd felt the right-front wheel slip into a pocket of mud. Without traction, he couldn't move the car any farther.

Several other men had left their cars and had run over to help. As they all attempted to push the car out of its muddy trap, Sam glanced up at the brightly lit house to the side of the parking area and hoped that Amanda wouldn't get into too much trouble without him.

WHEN EVAN FINISHED his conversation with the elderly man and started to walk away, Amanda knew she had to do something. Sam or no Sam, they couldn't afford to lose Evan again.

"Hello," she said, approaching him and smiling, as casually as if they'd just bumped into each other at a party and she had no idea who he really was.

"Hi." His brown eyes were so open and honest,

Amanda realized without a doubt that Sam was an excellent judge of character. For all they knew, Evan might even now have been working on a way to return the money to Sam. Or some of it, at least.

"What brings you to the party?" Evan asked, and Amanda decided to go along with the original story she'd started at the clinic today.

"My father," she said. "My husband and I are looking for a place that offers a little more than conventional Western medical treatment does."

"You won't be sorry," Evan replied. "The doctors had all but given up on my mother, but from what she told me today, she should be out in time to celebrate the New Year."

"That's fantastic," Amanda said, and meant it. "Do you mind if I ask you a few questions about the clinic?"

"Fire away," Evan replied, reaching for another glass of champagne.

"Is it terribly expensive?"

Several emotions crossed his face. Regret, she was certain of that. A flicker of pain. This man had not made the decision to run off with The Blackthorne Agency's money lightly.

"Yes. It's something of a financial commitment. But when you put that up against a human life—"

"I know," Amanda said, gently interrupting. She knew enough. She knew why this man had run off with the money. He'd been put in an untenable situation, and had reacted emotionally.

The only thing she couldn't understand was why Evan had thought Sam wouldn't help him. From everything Sam had told her, he considered Evan's mother to be like a member of his own family. But it had been

Evan's call, Evan's decision, and she couldn't pretend to read his mind or fathom his actions.

Now the only thing that mattered was making sure Sam had a chance to talk to Evan. Before he ran again.

SAM FINALLY REACHED the large stone veranda, and gratefully accepted a glass of punch from one of the waiters. He took a long, deep swallow, cooling his dry throat, then another. Then he glanced down at the mud speckling his pants, and grimaced.

Well, a few of the others who had helped him didn't look any better. Thank God it was a casual affair. And if anyone asked, he could simply say he'd had car trouble.

Now he had to find a bathroom before he made his entrance, and make sure that everything was in place. The last thing he needed was for Evan to see his mustache slowly sliding down his face.

He made the necessary repairs to his disguise, then sauntered into the main room just in time to see Evan take Amanda's arm and escort her to a table on the far side laden with various appetizers—cheese and crackers, several dips and the accompanying vegetables, chilled shrimp and cocktail sauce, tiny skewers of chicken and pork. And of course, the open bar.

But Sam didn't see any of this. He was too preoccupied with the sight of Amanda's hand tucked firmly into the crook of Evan's arm.

Sam wasn't jealous; he was simply astounded. How had Amanda managed to work so fast? Even as he thought this, he saw her look up at Evan and laugh, saw that long fall of blond hair catch the light from the crystal chandelier.

She amazed him.

He had to give her credit. When he hadn't come inside right away, she must have thought she needed to delay Evan. Make sure he stayed in plain sight. She was simply ensuring that he didn't run again.

Sam found himself relieved. Tonight was the night he wanted everything put to rest. He wanted to know what had happened; what had possessed Evan to run off with the agency's assets. He wanted, more than anything, to know why Evan hadn't confided in him.

As he approached Amanda and Evan, he took a deep breath. Confrontations were never easy, but this was one that had to be faced.

EVAN LOOKED UP AS Sam approached him. The expression in his dark brown eyes seemed sad. Almost mournful.

"Hello, Sam."

That stopped him in his tracks.

"Evan."

The two men stared at each other, both at a loss for words. Amanda glanced from one to the other.

Finally Sam cleared his throat and said, "I'm so sorry about your mother."

"Yeah." Evan couldn't seem to look at him. "But she's recovering."

"That's good. That's good." Sam studied his partner, wondering how to find the right words. *Why did you do it? Why didn't you come to me? At least talk to me?*

He didn't know what to say.

"Sam," Evan began. "Sam, I'm sorry. I just—when I found out—" He hesitated.

Sam glanced at Amanda, then back at his partner. He had to tread very carefully here.

"It must have been pretty overwhelming."

"It was. It was...the single hardest thing I've ever been through."

Sam considered this. It was probably true. Evan had led a rather uneventful life up until he and Sam had started working as private detectives. "Boring" and "dull" were two of the words Evan had actually used to describe his past.

"I didn't know what to do," Evan whispered, looking utterly miserable. And Sam realized that Evan still had no idea what he planned to do to him by way of punishment. Or how he wanted to be reimbursed.

Evan had stolen money from him. Technically, he hadn't done anything illegal, as the agency account had been in both their names. And he hadn't had to forge any documentation in order to clean out the account. But morally, it had been a damnable decision.

"You could have come to me," Sam said, keeping his voice low. "You could have talked to me, Evan, and let me know what was going on." What he wanted to say, what he needed to say, was that he didn't understand how Evan could ever have thought Sam wouldn't have given him the money.

"You don't understand," Evan said. "I'd already gone to several relatives. Distant relatives, but I thought I could use the agency, how well we were doing, as an assurance I'd pay the money back. But they all—they thought—they thought what I was going to do was ridiculous. Taking her down to Mexico, trying alternative methods of treatment—"

"I don't think it's ridiculous," Sam said. "I think you did a very good thing. You saved your mother's life. It's just the way you chose to do it that I have a little prob-

lem with." He took a deep breath, then forced the next
words out.

"Evan, you left me holding the bag."

AMANDA WATCHED SAM as the discussion quietly
progressed. And at each twist and turn, she admired
him more and more. He was gentle, but firm. He didn't
try to scare or threaten Evan, but he let him know he
didn't like what had been done.

Surely the two men could reach some sort of compromise. The important thing was, they were talking. Evan
wasn't running.

She was confident the future of The Blackthorne
Agency would be settled before the night was over.

IT TURNED OUT THAT EVAN hadn't used up nearly as
much of the money as Sam had suspected. He still had
quite a considerable chunk of it deposited in a bank in
San Diego. He was able to write Sam a check for half the
total amount he'd run off with. As he tore the check out
of his checkbook, Evan glanced up at Sam and made the
rather wistful promise that if he were ever in Los Angeles, he would drop in for a visit.

"What exactly are you planning on doing after your
mother gets back on her feet?" Sam said. The three of
them had adjourned to the terrace out back, where
lights from the main rooms illuminated the small table
where they sat.

"I don't know. Mother doesn't want to remain in
Mexico, even though she's come to really care for several of the people in the clinic. I thought we might move
back to southern California—"

"There's a job waiting for you if you want it," Sam said, the words surprising him as they left his mouth.

Evan looked as if he couldn't even begin to take in their meaning.

"Sam... You...you don't have to.... But it would mean so much—"

"I can't begin to approve of what you did," Sam said. The warm, expansive feeling around his heart told him he'd done the right thing. "But I can certainly understand being scared, and feeling as if that was the only way out."

Evan was overcome with emotion as he looked away, his throat working, his eyes filling. He blinked furiously, then tried to meet Sam's gaze.

"We'll be back in California right after the first of the year," he said, his voice hoarse.

"Okay." Sam glanced at Amanda, and wasn't surprised to see her blue eyes suspiciously bright. She had too much heart to be a P.I. But then, so did he, and it had never gotten him in that much trouble. Strange, how little trouble it took to actually be a decent human being; to try to understand why someone would do something. To practice a little compassion, in whatever way he could.

"Ready to go?" he asked her. He found that he suddenly wanted to be alone with Amanda, now that his reason for being down here in Puerto Vallarta was resolved. He wanted to be alone with her, to walk along the beach, to take her back to their room and make love to her.

"Yes." She turned toward Evan before she got up out of her chair. "It was very nice meeting you. I hope I'll see you again, Evan."

"You will," Evan said.

Class all the way, Sam thought as he admired Amanda. *And here I am, with mud on my pants*. Well, she'd accepted his proposal, and Amanda was smart enough to know that what she saw was exactly what she would get.

He thought about that as they headed down the steps, hand in hand, toward Ricardo's car. They'd done enough detective work for tonight. Now what they both needed was a little rest and relaxation. Amanda was such a special woman, the least he could do was show her a little romance.

11

A WALK ALONG THE BEACH at night seemed the least he could do. Sam wanted Amanda to remember this particular time in her life as being romantic.

They stayed close by the hotel, within range of its lights. Even though he didn't feel the area was unsafe after dark, one couldn't be too careful. Strange, how when he was around Amanda, his thoughts always came back to protecting her.

They walked along the beach, hand in hand, watching the moonlight glint across the ocean. Listening to the gentle hissing and crashing of the surf. Smelling that ocean smell—sharp, salty and tangy.

He liked the way she didn't mind the wind in her hair. He really liked that she preferred wearing it down. He couldn't resist the urge to touch it, run his fingers through it, then turn her gently in his arms and kiss her. And as always, when he kissed her, the world seemed to fade away, to be replaced by that sensual urgency, that desire to get as close as possible.

He didn't finish the kiss by urging her back to their room. Sam sensed they both needed a little time to unwind after the day they'd had. A stroll along the sand, breathing in the fresh night air, feeling the tropical breeze against their faces, watching the moonlight do its silvery dance on the water, seemed just the thing.

But anyplace in the world would be romantic with

Amanda by his side. Sam didn't voice his thoughts out loud; he was almost vaguely ashamed of them. They didn't seem to be the thoughts a man should have. Yet he knew they were true, and came from his heart. That shouldn't have surprised him.

He was a romantic at heart. Even his mother had often remarked on the fact. He was passionate about his work. He'd rescued Hercule when he'd been down on his luck. He liked to help people, and if he was honest with himself, he believed in the basic goodness of people.

He also believed that he and Amanda had a good chance—make that a great chance—at a happy marriage. Perhaps he wouldn't be able to keep her in the style she'd been accustomed to, but she wouldn't lack for love. He would have given her anything, and if good intentions and potential counted for anything, he had those by the bushel.

He looked down at her as they walked along the shoreline. Up ahead of them, another couple strolled, hand in hand. It was definitely a night for lovers.

"Sam?"

Her voice was so soft. He could listen to it forever.

"Yes?"

"These last two days... They've been the happiest days of my life."

Emotion swelled inside his chest, threatening to overwhelm him. He knew exactly what she meant.

"Me, too." He let go of her hand and brought his arm up around her shoulder, held her close. The gesture felt so warm, so natural with her. As did everything else.

"I've never felt...so *alive*."

"Yeah." There were so many things he wanted to say

to her, but he just didn't have the words. A poet he wasn't. But he knew what she felt, because he'd felt it, as well. What they'd shared in their hotel room—both the physical consummation of their feelings and the words they'd expressed—had changed him. He felt a great hope for his future. And a great happiness inside him.

"I wanted you to know, Sam. Because I've never felt this way with anyone else. And I know I never will."

He stopped then, put his arms around her again. "Oh, Amanda," he said, the words muffled as he touched his lips to the top of her head, her hair, then kissed her there. "Amanda, there's never been anyone like you."

Utter contentment. The peace of the moment. The gentle sighing of the surf, the soft caress of the ocean breeze, the smells and sounds of a tropical night—

The sound of footsteps running on the sand—

Too late, Sam looked up.

And saw Anton Black.

"Run!" he said to Amanda, giving her a push, then turning to face the detective and three other men.

"No! I won't leave you!" And damned if she didn't take the sandals she held in her hands and brandish them like knives, heels out, ready to fight.

"Anton!" Sam shouted. The tropical breeze seemed to diminish his words, whip them out to sea. "Don't do this!"

The detective stopped. He was a tall man, almost gaunt, with dark eyes and hair, and a mustache. The last time Sam had seen him, he'd been clean-shaven. Now he stood on the sand, in jeans and a black T-shirt, his eyes on Amanda, his mind undoubtedly on the reward Libby Hailey would offer him.

"Sam. How did you ever think you could hide her from me?" He smiled, and Sam didn't like the look in the man's eyes.

"We're married," Amanda said, still gripping the sandals. "There's nothing my mother can do about it."

Sam felt his heart beat crazily in his chest. They were married, if what had happened in that hotel room had meant anything at all. Now, because of what Amanda had just said, he knew it was true.

"Back off," he ordered, staring at each of the men in turn. "You don't have any business here. Leave my wife alone."

"Sam," Anton said softly, starting forward. "You should know that a little thing like marriage can be annulled. Especially when you're dealing with a woman like Libby Hailey."

Then they closed in.

HE CAME TO WITH A BLINDING pain in his head, and managed to stagger down the beach to Ricardo's hotel. The minute his friend saw him, he offered to call the police.

"No. I just have to get to the airport. Right now."

"You're in no shape to travel, my friend."

"It doesn't matter. I have to find her." Sam swallowed against the fear building in his throat. "Can you get me to a phone? I have to make a call."

"Of course."

Ricardo helped him around behind the front desk, then gave him a receiver after punching a few buttons.

Sam glanced at the clock overhead. The numbers

seemed to blur, but he could just make out the time. Three thirty-three in the morning.

They'd knocked him out but good.

Well, Nick would still be up. They'd discussed all sorts of contingencies, including what would happen if Anton found Amanda and kidnapped her. So Nick would know exactly what to do and whom to call.

Because at this point, there wasn't a second to waste.

THE FOLLOWING AFTERNOON, Sam let himself into his apartment above the nightclub. Every single muscle in his body ached, if that was possible.

But his heart hurt worst of all.

Some hero he'd been. Some protector. Some fiancé. He'd been seduced by the ocean breezes, the sound of the surf. He should have been on the alert for anyone and anything. They should have stayed in their room, they should never have gone to Mexico, they—

Should have, would have and *could have* could kill you in this life if you let those thoughts take over. Sam had learned from long and painful experience that sometimes all you could do was start from exactly where you were.

"Sam," Nick said, coming into the room. He was dressed in cutoffs and a muscle T, looking as if he'd just stepped off a surfboard.

"Yeah."

"Mrs. Boswell called."

"I can pick up Hercule later—"

"No, it's not about the dog. She knows where Amanda is."

"MY DEAR BOY," said Mrs. Boswell, "this entire affair is nothing short of *barbaric*."

"I won't argue with you there."

"First I lose my beloved Fifi, and now you have lost that darling girl. Well, I cannot stand aside and let this happen, so I decided to do a little calling around, and even though I absolutely detest the woman—"

"Start from the beginning," Sam interrupted, reaching for the pad of lined paper he always kept at his desk. "Don't leave anything out."

It turned out that Mrs. Boswell knew a dear friend of Libby Hailey's, a society matron named Mrs. Rugglesworth. She and her husband were filthy rich, so Libby adored them. They'd been invited to the wedding, but Mr. Rugglesworth had business in New York and he just couldn't get away, so his wife had wanted company at the wedding. Someone to go with her. Mrs. Boswell had declined.

"Can't stand the woman," she said now. "Lynette's a hopeless gossip. Her husband's millions were the worst thing that could have happened to her. She never had to marshal her resources and do a thing with her own life. She takes far too much delight in others' misfortunes, but her life is always 'absolutely *fab*-ulous,' as she says."

"I know the type."

"Lying through her teeth. Anyway, she called me this morning and told me the wedding is being pushed up. Libby told her Marvin's business demands it. She begged me to come with her, because she hates to fly—"

"Fly? Since when do you have to fly to a wedding in Beverly Hills? Am I missing something?"

"Oh, no, dear boy. Libby is holding the wedding at a friend's mansion, just outside Las Vegas. Very hush-hush, you know. Quickly thrown together. It was supposed to be scheduled for Christmas Eve, but they're going ahead with it this weekend."

"I'll be damned."

"Now, I know Amanda belongs with you, Sam. Libby is probably threatening her, or worse."

"I have to get there," Sam said, already starting to make plans.

"Now, now, I'm already ahead of you. When Nick called and told me you were coming back, I asked him why he sounded so upset. He said you'd given him permission to tell me everything—"

"Of course."

"And so I went ahead and told Lynette I'd be delighted to come with her, and we could even use my private jet, but on the condition that my two dogs, Fifi and Hercule, came with me."

"And?" Sam prompted, leaning forward, knowing this had to be leading somewhere.

"I read this once in a mystery. Worked like a charm, how that detective got inside in order to find some clues." She paused, clearly delighted by her cleverness. "You, Sam, are going to pose as Jean-Paul, my beloved pets' lifestyle consultant and personal trainer."

SAM SUPPOSED THINGS could have been worse.

He couldn't think of quite how at the moment, but he was sure they could have been.

Mrs. Boswell's jet had taken off from Santa Monica airport that morning, and the forty-five minute flight to Las Vegas had been largely uneventful. If you didn't count getting up half-a-dozen times to supply both Hercule and Fifi with bottled water and gourmet biscuits an event.

Oh, and adjusting their sweaters. After all, the plane was air-conditioned.

And playing with them. Both dogs had quite a cache of toys, courtesy of Mrs. Boswell. Hercule and Fifi had just finished an exhausting game of "get the shoe."

"You're going to pay for this," Sam muttered to Hercule. The French bulldog looked patently ridiculous in that sweater with the cherries and the red leather leash-and-collar set. Mrs. Boswell had completed the outfit with a bright red, crocheted beret.

"Very French, wouldn't you say?" she'd remarked. "So smart this time of year."

Hercule had merely grinned, loving the attention. Sam thought he looked like a small bat playing dress-up.

Now Sam watched as Mrs. Boswell made her way down the length of the jet, absolutely beaming.

"Lynette's beside herself," she whispered as she sat down next to Sam. "Do you know she actually asked me if I was sleeping with you? Imagine me, having an affair with a young man your age!"

He could tell the idea tickled her immensely.

She patted his arm. "Don't worry. There's a bridal lunch the day before the wedding, and Lynette and I are invited. I'll make sure you get inside the gate, if you get my drift. You'll see Amanda this afternoon."

At the mention of her name, Hercule yipped.

"Yes, you will," Mrs. Boswell said, rubbing the wrinkled head.

"Thank you," Sam said quietly. "I don't know how I can ever begin to thank you."

"You gave me back my Fifi," she said, hugging the white toy poodle close. "That was more than enough."

THEY LANDED IN LAS VEGAS, and went to the Luxor to shower and dress. Then, within two hours of their arrival, Sam found himself in a white stretch limousine, with Mrs. Boswell, Mrs. Rugglesworth, Fifi, and an ecstatic Hercule.

Hercule loved to ride in the car. The little bulldog had almost gone into cardiac arrest when he'd comprehended that he was going to be allowed inside a limousine.

"Now, behave yourself," Sam said, his voice low. "You can't let on that you know Amanda."

Hercule whined.

"Just try to act—oh, hell, just try not to be too obvious, okay?"

The dog cocked his head, his beret askew.

Sam glanced out the window as the desert scenery sped by. Wherever they were going, it was truly a little ways out of town. Isolated. The perfect place for Libby to do her dirty work.

He had the element of surprise on his side. And disguise. For his role as Jean-Paul, he'd slicked his hair straight back from his forehead with a pomade, donned a thin mustache, and created a little more of a nose. Skillful makeup had concealed the worst of the bruises Anton Black had given him. Dressed in a simple pair of black pants and a white poet's shirt, he looked the part of a smart and effete animal expert.

Fifi was exquisitely trained, and would help him play the part. But Hercule—

Well, he would just have to go for it. Improvise.

"Too bad Amanda isn't here with us," he muttered to the happily panting bulldog. "She could probably speak your language, too."

MRS. BOSWELL LET HER friend get out first, then leaned over and whispered to Sam, "I've instructed the driver to stay here for the next few hours, and to make sure he doesn't get hemmed in with other cars. He's at your service if you and Amanda choose to make a quick escape."

"I should offer you a job with the agency. You're that good."

She beamed. "You don't live as long as I have without picking up a thing or two."

INSIDE THE MANSION, Sam quickly deduced a few things. This particular mansion looked like something out of 1001 Arabian Nights; lush, opulent, almost decadent. And strangely enough, the assembled crowd of almost eighty people, though gathered in the desert, were all dressed as elegantly as if they were attending a grand wedding at an English church amid green lawns and flower-filled gardens.

However, there was no sign of Amanda.

This particular prenuptial event had been put together in a flash, but still looked lovely, thanks to Libby's considerable talents as a lifestyle coordinator.

And, last but not least, the cake on display toward the front of the gloriously beautiful enclosed courtyard looked rather elaborate for a prewedding bridal luncheon.

His suspicions were confirmed when Libby walked to the front of the seated crowd.

"Ladies! Gentlemen! It's my pleasure to inform you that I've moved the wedding up one day. There is no luncheon, you're here for the actual event."

Sam felt his heart slam in his chest. He couldn't believe what he was hearing. Libby had to be desperate, to be making this kind of move. Why hadn't Amanda contacted him? Run away?

But where? The estate was as effectively isolated as a house in one of those Phyllis Whitney novels his sisters had loved. Where would Amanda have gone? Sam was positive Libby wouldn't have given her daughter access to a phone. Perhaps she'd even threatened her.

A million dollars could make even a perfectly reasonable person do strange things.

Now, he watched in horror as Marvin Burgess stepped up to a flower-bedecked "altar," and a young man sat down at an electric keyboard and began to play the opening notes of the wedding march.

Then Sam craned his head with everyone else in order to get a first glimpse of the bride.

AMANDA DIDN'T KNOW WHAT she was going to do, but she knew she wasn't going to marry Marvin. She couldn't. She'd only been stalling for time because her mother had threatened to send Anton Black after Sam and "arrange a little accident."

She had to talk to Sam. Figure out what to do. Her mother hadn't allowed a phone in her vicinity, and Amanda hadn't dared call Sam because she didn't want any harm to come to him.

All she was sure of today was that nothing on the face of this earth could force her to stand before God and everyone else and say "I do." Her mother couldn't make her do anything in front of a crowd. And Amanda knew this gave her the upper hand, because she wasn't opposed to creating a huge scene.

It was her life, after all. Hers and Sam's.

Not even bothering with a smile, she started down the outdoor runner, one step at a time.

HIS HEART TURNED OVER when he saw her.

She didn't look happy. In fact, she looked so achingly vulnerable that his heart went out to her. He wanted to get out of his seat, run to her, take her into his arms and tell her she didn't have to marry anyone.

Clearly, Libby had done something to frighten her daughter. And why wouldn't she? There was a cool million at stake. He wondered if she had informed Amanda of that particular fact.

He glanced at Mrs. Boswell, Fifi sitting contentedly on her lap. The older woman looked as horrified as he felt.

She leaned over and whispered in his ear, "You'll have to do something quick. No time for careful planning now!"

"You're right. I may have to take you up on the limousine, after all." And with that, Sam began to undress a struggling Hercule as he formulated a last-minute plan.

"DEARLY BELOVED, we are gathered here...."

Sam thought quickly as the minister droned on. Marvin had taken Amanda's hand possessively in his own, but she had yet to meet his eyes. Strange, how no one in the audience seemed to react to that, or think it was odd. Most brides beamed up at their grooms, tears of joy in their eyes.

Not with a mask of utter dejection and despair.

"And so, if there is anyone here who has any objections to this man and woman being joined together in holy matrimony, speak now or—"

"One minute!" Sam shot to his feet, Hercule tucked neatly beneath his arm. Remembering who he was supposed to be, a Frenchman who created lifestyles for pampered pooches, he called out, "I have a doggie with zee heatstroke!"

"What?" The minister, clearly perplexed, stared at Sam.

He saw his chance and took it. Muttering apologies as he left his seat, Sam quickly reached the aisle and then headed toward the bride and groom.

"Zees doggie, he ees zuffering! Zuffering, I tell you! Look at zee fur, it ees black, *black!* Do you not understand? Black, though it ees a classic color, and Coco Chanel approved, it holds zee heat, and we must help zee leetle fellow before zees marriage can go on!"

Sam had addressed his remarks to the minister, and now he turned toward the assembled audience, knowing his French accent was utterly appalling and about as authentic as a painting on velvet posing as a Renoir. Yet he had no choice but to go on. "Ees there a doctor in zee house?"

Amanda's facial expression transformed right before his eyes. She recognized first Hercule, then him, and beneath the lovely veil he saw hope flare in those blue eyes.

Marvin clearly sensed trouble. "I say, this is highly irregular—"

Sam knew he was in trouble. So much for Jean-Paul, the Frenchman.

Create a distraction. A doozy.

Sam set Hercule down on the ground, close to Marvin. "Hercule," he whispered. "Get the shoe! Get the shoe!" This was said while eyeing Marvin's tasteful Bruno Magli shoes.

Hercule glanced at his owner, doubtful.

Terrific. The one time he decides to obey me, and not chew on real shoes.

"It's okay, Hercule. *Get the shoe!*"

The bulldog went for it, charging at Marvin, grabbing at his shoes as the man shrieked and danced about. Then Hercule, in true bulldog fashion, grabbed a large jawful of his Armani tuxedo pant leg and hung on for dear life, shaking his head and play-growling low in his throat.

"Mad dog!" a guest called out.

"Rabies!" cried another.

"Sam!" said Amanda.

"You!" screamed Libby, approaching quickly.

Sam thought even quicker. He leaned over, grabbed Amanda's hand, and started down the aisle. "Hate to leave so quickly, Padre," he called back toward the minister, "but we have a wedding to catch."

"Hercule!" Amanda cried, and Sam glanced back, realizing he couldn't leave his dog at the mercy of Libby Hailey. As if on cue, the minister leaned down, managed to disengage Hercule from Marvin's pant leg, and tossed the little French bulldog to the side in complete and utter panic.

All eyes watched as the dog sailed through the air, happily panting, clearly thinking this was all part of a new game. All eyes watched as he landed squarely on the top layer of the elaborate wedding cake, and the top and middle layers exploded down into the base in a huge mass of fluffy white cake and rich decorator frosting.

Dead silence.

Hercule lay completely still in the totally ruined cake.

Sam's heart almost stopped.

Then everyone watched as the bulldog's head broke through the mass of ruined confection, his funny little smashed-in face covered with frosting, his buggy eyes blinking. He barked sharply, once, twice, as if to say, "Now *that* was fun, let's do it again!"

"Hercule!" Amanda called.

The little dog sprang into action, but not before Libby instructed a butler, who seemed to be trying not to laugh, to grab the dog.

He did.

Hercule, being carted off and thinking this was all part of a new game, turned in the man's arms and began to furiously lick his face, smearing him with frosting in the process. The butler, unable to see, tripped and lost his balance, dropping the dog. Hercule ran to the table next to the one that now held the ruined cake, and grabbed the corner of the classic white linen tablecloth. He tugged once, twice, in ecstasy over this new game.

The elaborate, swan ice sculpture teetered.

The gorgeous fountain made up of champagne glasses tinkled slightly in the totally still air.

Everyone watched, no one able to tear their eyes away.

"Damn you!" Libby screeched, as she headed toward the bulldog.

Hercule, who had been just about to drop the cloth, panicked at the sight of Libby and ran, the cloth still in his locked jaws.

The swan teetered, and finally crashed in an explosion of shattering, crystalline ice shards.

The champagne fountain tipped, swayed, then one, then another of the bottom glasses fell over. Once the foundation broke, the entire pyramid came crashing down, glasses flying—luckily, all very nice plastic because, as Libby Hailey had once said on *Libby's World*, "Why, the plastic glasses they have now for outdoor weddings are so nice, there's no reason to be embarrassed to use them."

Sam turned toward Amanda. While everyone else had been watching Hercule's antics with breathless anticipation, she'd been struggling with the fastening of her bridal gown.

He understood immediately.

"Allow me."

Buttons were unbuttoned, and to Sam's complete astonishment and admiration, Amanda coolly stepped out of the elaborate gown, and stood in the bright sunshine, clad in nothing but the most gorgeous, cream-colored silk slip he'd ever seen, her high heels, and the veil.

This time, his heart really almost stopped.

She draped the dress carefully over a chair, then tugged at the incredibly large diamond ring on her finger.

"Marvin!" she called.

He looked up, a miserable man, upset over his torn tuxedo.

She tossed her engagement ring to him, the enormous diamond glinting in the desert sun.

He caught it, and the look he gave Amanda left no one present in any doubt as to the state of their union.

Libby was still by the table, throwing an absolute fit over her ruined cake, her shattered swan, and the masses of plastic champagne flutes scattered everywhere.

"Hercule!" Sam yelled. It was time to get out of Dodge.

The bulldog, still covered with frosting, rocketed into his arms. Sam caught him, tucked him beneath his arm, grabbed Amanda's hand, and they started to run.

They didn't stop as they entered the large mansion, raced toward the front door, then down the steps and outside, all the way past the long line of parked cars until they reached Mrs. Boswell's limousine at the end of the street.

Sam glanced back. Amanda looked beautiful, a hectic color in her cheeks, the short silk slip molded to her body and showing off a considerable length of leg, her veil flying wildly.

He flung open the door, tossed a happily wiggling Hercule in, then Amanda, and got in himself, calling to the driver, "Take me to a chapel."

"You got it, boss," he replied as he turned on the ignition.

THEY STOPPED at the very first wedding chapel they came to on the Strip. Amanda had all her necessary IDs, as she'd tucked them inside her bra before the ceremony at the mansion had begun. She'd intended to walk out on that wedding, no matter what.

Before they even entered the tacky little Vegas chapel, Sam had the driver radio for another limousine to take Mrs. Boswell and Mrs. Rugglesworth safely back to their hotel.

Inside, before two witnesses who looked surprisingly weepy for total strangers, Sam said the words that would bind him to Amanda for the rest of his life, a woman he'd met two weeks ago.

There were no false starts. No hesitations. Sam Cooper, a scruffy, down-on-his-luck P.I., who had believed he was doomed to be a lifelong bachelor, discovered that taking that leap of faith and getting married was surprisingly easy when you found the right woman. The only one.

Amanda repeated her vows, and Sam started to laugh.

"What?" she asked, her blue eyes shining with happiness.

"You have frosting on your nose."

"You'll have to kiss it off, then."

The minister cleared his throat, and they both looked at him. "I now pronounce you husband and wife." He eyed Sam pointedly. "You may kiss the bride."

Sam let out a whoop of delight, took the elaborate bouquet of cream-colored roses and ivy out of Amanda's arms and tossed it. Hercule raced after the flowers and starting to drag them back down the red-carpeted aisle toward the happy couple. Then Sam swept Amanda into a low dip and kissed her senseless.

THE LIMOUSINE DRIVER took them back to the Luxor, and Sam carried Amanda inside while people all around them whooped and hollered. Sam wasn't sure if it was because they so obviously looked "just married," or if it was the sight of a stunningly beautiful woman dressed in nothing but a silk slip.

It didn't matter. Nothing could ruin this day.

They stopped at the first boutique they found, and he bought Amanda two outfits.

"As much as I like seeing you running around half-naked, we could get ourselves arrested," he told her.

When he saw the worried frown on her face as he whipped out his charge card, he whispered, "Relax."

"Sam, it's so expensive—"

"And I can cover it," he said. Even though Evan's check hadn't had a chance to clear the bank yet, Mrs. Boswell had rewarded him handsomely for finding Fifi.

"Now," he said, as they headed out into the hotel lobby toward the registration desk, "we have to find ourselves a room, because what I have planned for you shouldn't have an audience."

She laughed.

They were at the desk, finalizing things with a clerk, when a familiar voice floated through the crowd.

"No, no, Sam! Not on your honeymoon. I insist!" Mrs. Boswell grabbed the pen out of his hand before he could finish filling out the registration slip and said to the startled clerk, "I want you to give these two charming young people the most elaborate honeymoon package this hotel has! Your best champagne on ice, and dinner for two! Make that three!" she said, patting Hercule. "And you must certainly put it on my account." She turned to Sam and Amanda. "Consider it my wedding present to the two of you."

"Mrs. Boswell, you can't—" Sam began.

"Nonsense! I have an obscene amount of money, and I love to spend it making people happy. Now, all you two have to promise me is that you'll make every attempt to make a go of things, and be happy." She smiled up at them, teary-eyed. "I do so want the two of you to be happy."

Sam put his arm around the elderly lady and gave her a hug. "Oh, I think we can promise that."

THE FIRST ORDER OF business in the luxurious honeymoon suite was giving a very sticky Hercule a complete shampoo.

The second was what newlyweds have done since the beginning of time. Only now it was different, Sam thought, because now she truly belonged to him. Now they would never be separated again. He thought of this as he kissed her, as he shaped her body with his hands, and as he finally slid inside her, his heart behind every single move he made.

He watched her find pleasure and, ultimately, her release, all the while his heart so full of feeling. And when he found his own, it was different this time, because he knew he would be waking up next to her for the rest of his life.

Just before he drifted off to sleep, he remembered something else his wise old mom had taught him, and quietly offered up a prayer of thanks.

Because Sam knew, from personal experience, how very easy it was to lose someone. Or never even find them in the first place.

SHE WAS HALF AWAKE the morning after their wedding, drifting in that delicious world of dreams. And she thought about how she wanted to sketch her husband's strong, handsome face. And the faces of all their children, whenever they should choose to arrive.

But before all that, she and Sam would have their first Christmas together. And every Christmas after that...

She opened her eyes and found him watching her, then loved the look of delight in his expression the instant he saw she was awake. Hercule snored softly at the foot of the king-size bed, exhausted after yesterday's rampage.

"Sam," she said, touching his cheekbone gently. "Those bruises..."

"They were all worth it," he said. "Each one. But I don't want to remember any of it. Let's start over." He smiled at her, a possessive gleam in his eyes. "Good morning, Mrs. Cooper," Sam said softly.

That voice thrilled her down to the tips of her toes.

"Good morning, Mr. Cooper," she replied.

"Sleep well?" he said.

"Barely."

He laughed.

"But I was thinking—"

She almost laughed out loud at the concerned expression that wrinkled his forehead. How he worried about her.

"I was thinking that when we get back to Malibu, I could help you with your work—"

"I don't think so, Amanda, because—"

"I thought I showed a real talent for detective work down in Mexico, and I—"

"There's no doubt about it, but—" He stopped. She knew her disappointment had to be obvious, and she also knew he couldn't bear to hurt her.

"How about," he said slowly, "if we take on various cases together? Just so we can sort of watch each other's backs?"

She smiled, relieved. "That's exactly what I was thinking. Because, you know, two people are always more powerful than one. It's better that way."

He thought of all the joy she'd brought into his life. All the joy and sheer, unadulterated *fun* they would have in the years to come. And he smiled.

"For once," he whispered, just before he covered her mouth in a kiss, "I agree with you."

THE MEN OF BACHELOR CREEK

Alaska. A place where men could be men—and women were scarce!

To Tanner, Joe and Hawk, Alaska was the final frontier. They'd gone to the ends of the earth to flee the one thing they all feared—MATRIMONY. Little did they know that three intrepid heroines would brave the wilds to "save" them from their lonely bachelor existences.

Enjoy

**#662 CAUGHT UNDER
THE MISTLETOE!**
December 1997

#670 DODGING CUPID'S ARROW!
February 1998

#678 STRUCK BY SPRING FEVER!
April 1998

by Kate Hoffmann

Available wherever Harlequin books are sold.

Take 4 bestselling love stories FREE

Plus get a FREE surprise gift!

Special Limited-time Offer

Mail to Harlequin Reader Service®

3010 Walden Avenue
P.O. Box 1867
Buffalo, N.Y. 14240-1867

YES! Please send me 4 free Harlequin Temptation® novels and my free surprise gift. Then send me 4 brand-new novels every month, which I will receive before they appear in bookstores. Bill me at the low price of $2.90 each plus 25¢ delivery and applicable sales tax, if any.* That's the complete price and a savings of over 10% off the cover prices—quite a bargain! I understand that accepting the books and gift places me under no obligation ever to buy any books. I can always return a shipment and cancel at any time. Even if I never buy another book from Harlequin, the 4 free books and the surprise gift are mine to keep forever.

142 BPA A3UP

Name	(PLEASE PRINT)	
Address	Apt. No.	
City	State	Zip

This offer is limited to one order per household and not valid to present Harlequin Temptation® subscribers. *Terms and prices are subject to change without notice. Sales tax applicable in N.Y.

UTEMP-696

©1990 Harlequin Enterprises Limited

HARLEQUIN® *Temptation*

It's a dating wasteland out there! So what's a girl to do when there's not a marriage-minded man in sight? Go hunting, of course.

Manhunting

Enjoy the hilarious antics of five intrepid heroines, determined to lead Mr. Right to the altar—whether he wants to go or not!

#669 *Manhunting in Memphis—*
Heather MacAllister (February 1998)

#673 *Manhunting in Manhattan—*
Carolyn Andrews (March 1998)

#677 *Manhunting in Montana—*
Vicki Lewis Thompson (April 1998)

#681 *Manhunting in Miami—*
Alyssa Dean (May 1998)

#685 *Manhunting in Mississippi—*
Stephanie Bond (June 1998)

She's got a plan—to find herself a man!

Available wherever Harlequin books are sold.

DEBBIE MACOMBER

invites you to the

★ HEART OF TEXAS ★

Join Debbie Macomber as she brings you the lives
and loves of the folks in the ranching community
of Promise, Texas.

If you loved Midnight Sons—don't miss
Heart of Texas! A brand-new six-book series
from Debbie Macomber.

Available in February 1998
at your favorite retail store.

Heart of Texas by Debbie Macomber

Lonesome Cowboy	February '98
Texas Two-Step	March '98
Caroline's Child	April '98
Dr. Texas	May '98
Nell's Cowboy	June '98
Lone Star Baby	July '98

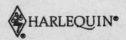

HARLEQUIN®

HPHRT1

KEY TO MY HEART

Unlock the secrets of romance just in time for the most romantic day of the year— Valentine's Day!

Key to My Heart features three of your favorite authors,

Kasey Michaels,
Rebecca York
and Muriel Jensen,

to bring you wonderful tales of romance and Valentine's Day dreams come true.

As an added bonus you can receive Harlequin's special Valentine's Day necklace. FREE with the purchase of every *Key to My Heart* collection.

Available in January, wherever Harlequin books are sold.

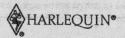

Free Gift Offer

With a Free Gift proof-of-purchase
from any Harlequin® book, you can receive
a beautiful cubic zirconia pendant.

This stunning marquise-shaped stone is a genuine cubic
zirconia—accented by an 18" gold tone necklace.
(Approximate retail value $19.95)

Send for yours today...
compliments of HARLEQUIN®

To receive your free gift, a cubic zirconia pendant, send us one original proof-of-
purchase, photocopies not accepted, from the back of any Harlequin Romance®, Harlequin
Presents®, Harlequin Temptation®, Harlequin Superromance®, Harlequin Love & Laughter®,
Harlequin Intrigue®, Harlequin American Romance®, or Harlequin Historicals® title
available at your favorite retail outlet, together with the Free Gift Certificate, plus a check or
money order for $1.65 U.S./$2.15 CAN. (do not send cash) to cover postage and handling,
payable to Harlequin Free Gift Offer. We will send you the specified gift. Allow 6 to 8 weeks
for delivery. Offer good until March 31, 1998, or while quantities last. Offer valid in the U.S.
and Canada only.

Free Gift Certificate

Name: _____

Address: _____

City: _____ State/Province: _____ Zip/Postal Code: _____

Mail this certificate, one proof-of-purchase and a check or money order for postage and
handling to: HARLEQUIN FREE GIFT OFFER 1998. In the U.S.: 3010 Walden Avenue, P.O.
Box 9071, Buffalo NY 14269-9057. In Canada: P.O. Box 604, Fort Erie, Ontario L2Z 5X3.

FREE GIFT OFFER   084-KEZ

ONE PROOF-OF-PURCHASE
To collect your fabulous FREE GIFT, a cubic zirconia pendant, you must include this
original proof-of-purchase for each gift with the properly completed Free Gift Certificate.

084-KEZR2